BRIGHT SHADOW

BRIGHT SHADOW

by AVI

※ ※ ※
※ ※

BRADBURY PRESS · New York

Bradbury Press
An Affiliate of Macmillan, Inc.
866 Third Avenue, New York, N.Y. 10022
Collier Macmillan Canada, Inc.
Manufactured in the United States of America
10 9 8 7 6 5 4 3 2 1
The text of this book is set in 12 pt. Janson

Library of Congress Cataloging in Publication Data:
Avi, 1937–   Bright shadow.
Summary: Having used four of the five wishes she is granted
to make on behalf of the hapless citizens of her country,
Morwenna flees the kingdom to decide what to do with the
last wish.
1. Children's stories, American.   [1. Fantasy]
I. Title.
PZ7.A953Br   1985   [Fic]   85-5719
ISBN 0-02-707750-0

For Coppélia

When bright, it's dark, when darkest, it's gone.
When gone for good, so are you.

What am I?

When dark, it's bright, when brightest, it's gone.
When gone for good, so will I be.

What am I?

✳

YOU HAVE FOUND ME.
After all these years I've been expecting
someone. I'm not even surprised it's you.
But before you ask for what you've come so
far to have, you must learn everything that
happened. It took many years for me to
learn everything. You must know it all . . .
now.

Listen then, for this is the story.

I

WHEN the country of . . . No, the name doesn't matter. It was long ago. It's different now and you know its name. But then, when the country began, there were five hundred wishes in the land. These were wishes that worked, you see, and they were used and cared for by a wizard.

Over the centuries, as one wizard succeeded another, unused wishes were passed on until by the time Pindel became Wizard only thirty-three wishes were left. During his life—he lived nearly a thousand years—Pindel had used twenty-eight wishes. Now only five were left. And Pindel was deathly ill.

The longer he lay alone the more he feared he would die without a successor. He *must* pass on the last wishes to someone who could use them well, someone rich in years, wisdom and experience.

Surely, he thought, the one to have the wishes should be the ruler of the land. Not that Pindel knew anything about the current king—or was it queen? He had been sick too long to know.

Summoning his remaining strength, Pindel rose from his bed of straw. Slowly, painfully, he made his way to the fortress palace and inched his way toward the throne room. Just as he approached, the throne room doors burst open. Out rushed Ruthvin, the king.

K ING Ruthvin was a small, lean man, hard and tight as if put together with wire bits. In one hand he held a short whip. In the other, a just-delivered message.

Pindel tried to catch the king's attention, but Ruthvin, intent upon that message, hurried past. Suddenly he stopped and turned back. Pindel, who was bent and ancient and dressed in rotting rags, seemed no more than a beggar to him.

"You are in the presence of the king," Ruthvin

snapped at the old man. "My law requires you to bow when I pass by."

With much pain and with trembling lips, Pindel slowly spoke. "I am the Wizard," he said. "I have lived for a thousand years. Now I am dying. But there are five wishes still within me. I must pass them on." Pindel reached toward the king with shaking hands.

Ruthvin had stopped listening. The message from his army chief was of far greater importance to him than the mumblings of some old man.

"What's that?" he muttered, not even looking at Pindel.

"Wishes . . ." Pindel answered, his strength ebbing. "I have the last five wishes to give . . ." He moved to touch the king.

Recoiling with disgust, Ruthvin lashed out at Pindel's hand with the butt of his whip. "If you have something to give me," he said, "be quick about it. I've no time to waste."

Pindel faltered, horrified. His hand was bleeding.

"Stand aside," barked the king, out of patience. "I've an important audience to hold."

Pindel tried to reach the king's sleeve. He wasn't fast enough. Ruthvin knocked him against the wall and strode away without a backward glance.

"The wishes!" gasped Pindel. "They must not be lost. They must be passed on." But no one was there to hear him. The king had already gone.

Slowly, his eyes dimming, Pindel slid to the floor unconscious.

WHY Morwenna left the throne room she never could recall—perhaps on some small, unimportant errand for Miss Helga, the chamber maid. Perhaps she went for a dusting cloth. Perhaps it was a bucket . . . All she remembers is that when she did go into the hallway she found the oldest man she had ever seen.

He was sitting on the floor, propped against the wall. His hair was as white and fine as mist, his skin was like the bark of an old tree, with arms, legs and fingers the brittle branches. One of his hands was bloody. His face, with eyes closed, was pale with pain. He appeared near death.

Morwenna didn't know what to do. Upset, she first looked toward the throne room. Then she looked at the old man. She wanted to run away. But moved by the man's wretchedness, she reached down and touched his arm.

"Please, sir," she said, uncomfortable at being so close. "Can I help?"

Pindel struggled to open his eyes and looked up. "Who are you?" he asked so faintly Morwenna could hardly hear him.

"My name is Morwenna," she said. "Miss Helga the chamber maid is close by. I'll get her if you'd like."

Pindel stared at Morwenna with deep, sad eyes. Suddenly, he snatched one of her hands. Where he found the strength, Morwenna didn't know, but it was impossible for her to move. And his gaze was so intense that Morwenna, no matter how much she wanted to, could not turn away.

In a low, mournful voice, Pindel began to speak. A sweet voice, a soft voice, almost a singing voice, it filled Morwenna with cutting cold.

"The last wishes are here. They will bring thee long life if thou keep thyself from harm, but

*nothing for thyself. Use them well. Waste them
not. Keep them and thyself well hid. Tell no
one what thou hast or before thy time* all, *both
thee and they, shall be lost. For when the
wishes are gone, so too shall thee be.*"

These words—so odd, so faint—made little
sense to Morwenna. Besides, even as she tried
to understand, Pindel, with his free hand, began to tap his fingertips on her open palm, once,
twice, five times in all. At the fifth touch she
felt very strange. It was as if . . . . as if she were
hollowed out. For the smallest part of a second
a sweet warmth ran through her. Then the feeling was gone.

And Pindel? When he had touched Morwenna for the fifth and final time, he released
his grip. With pitiful, tearful eyes, he studied
her.

"Forgive me," she heard him say. "Forgive
. . . ." Then she saw him slump forward and
die.

Terribly frightened, Morwenna wanted to
run. Something drew her back. She looked at
the stone floor where Pindel had been. Nothing
was there but a small pile of dust. A faint whispering wind lingered a moment in the air.

Bewildered by what had been done and said—
if anything had been done or said—Morwenna
stood absolutely still.

*T*HE audience to which King Ruthvin had
gone with such haste was requested by
his army chief, Sibald. He was a sweating, nervous man who lived his life in service to his
king.

Once Ruthvin had seated himself, Sibald
bowed low. Then he quickly informed His
Majesty that the people were growing more
restless than usual.

"Why?" demanded the king.

"High taxes, beatings, the cost of bread."

With a wave of his whip, the king dismissed
it all. "There's nothing new in that."

"Majesty," said Sibald, "do you remember
some time ago I informed you about a band of
rebels that attempted to seize a granary?"

"We caught them and had them executed,"
said the king.

"And those peasants who tried to take back
their land . . ."

"Still in prison," said the king.

"Uprisings like these," said Sibald, "are being reported with increasing frequency."

"What of it?" returned the king.

Sibald drew a deep breath. "Majesty, there appears to be a belief among the poorest of people that when life becomes unbearable, someone will come to save them."

"I am ready to deal with anyone."

"Majesty," continued Sibald, "the tradition kept alive by these people is that the person shall come along and save them with . . . wishes."

Something stirred in Ruthvin's mind.

"Those who believe this story," Sibald hurried on, "say that somewhere—no one knows where—there is an all-powerful wizard, a man who holds the only wishes in the land. Some say he holds a million. Others say it's few. Though he has not been seen or heard of for years, people have actually begun searching for him."

"And?" said the king, growing upset.

"My spies tell me there is a rumor that this man is about, here, *now*."

"You did say . . . wishes?" asked the king.

"I did," Sibald replied.

"Today . . . just moments ago," said the king, speaking slowly and flexing his whip in his hands, "I met a man . . . who offered me . . . wishes. Five of them . . ."

"Majesty!" Sibald gasped, almost too afraid to speak. "Did you accept?"

The whip snapped in two. "No."

"Majesty, even if the story is untrue, even if the man you met lied, the idea that somebody is claiming to be this wizard may do great harm. There are other bands of rebels about. They all are small, timid, afraid to show themselves. But such a man as you met might fool people, make them believe they could oppose you with his help. It could be dangerous."

King Ruthvin tried to remember what the beggar looked like. But he had paid so little attention to the man, all he could recall was that his clothing was old.

"Where," Sibald asked timidly, "did you see this man?"

Instead of answering, King Ruthvin sprang to his feet. With Sibald close behind, the king hurried to the spot where he had met the beggar. All they found was a pile of dust.

The king kicked open the throne room doors. He found Miss Helga the chamber maid and, off in the corner, Morwenna. Both were dusting.

"Did someone come into this throne room?" he demanded.

Miss Helga spun about. Realizing it was the king, she curtsied hastily.

"A poor man, you fool!" the king cried. "A beggar! Anyone! Answer me!"

"No, Your Majesty," she said. "No one at all."

Slamming the doors behind them, King Ruthvin and Sibald hurried toward the palace courtyard. They had only one thought between them: they must catch this man who claimed to to be a wizard. He had become the king's enemy.

A s soon as King Ruthvin and his army chief rushed off, the chamber maid turned to Morwenna.

"Morwenna," she scolded, "the law says you must stand and bow before the king. He's beaten people with less excuse. You're lucky he didn't notice."

Miss Helga was a plump, strong, good-natured woman who usually scolded to cover a soft heart. Morwenna had worked for the chamber maid, even lived with her during the work week, for more than a year, and had grown very fond of her.

Normally, they chatted as they worked. But when Morwenna came back from meeting Pindel, she felt so strange, so unsure about what—if anything—had happened, that she hadn't said a word.

In the time since, she had done very little but think and puzzle. How ancient the man had been, but . . . the more she thought of him . . . how beautifully ancient. And he had touched her hand in such an odd way, had made her feel so different. As for his words . . . they had been said too faintly, too quickly. The only thing she understood—or thought she understood—was that he said he was giving her five wishes. It was all such a jumble, her head began to ache. She decided she had to speak.

"I did see someone," she admitted. "Just outside the doors."

"For heaven's sake!" exclaimed Miss Helga. "Who?"

"An old man."

"Then you should have spoken," the chamber maid said. "It seemed important. What was he doing?"

"He . . . he talked to me . . . about . . . wishes," said Morwenna, embarrassed.

Miss Helga threw up her arms in exasperation. "Wishes!" she cried. "And you almost thirteen. Such nonsense, girl." But she looked at Morwenna with curiosity. "What exactly did he say?"

Morwenna thought a moment. "I'm not sure," she said.

Miss Helga began to lecture across the throne room, telling Morwenna that people like them— hard-working people—had no time or place in their lives for fairy tales. It was a waste to think such things. Yet once again she asked, "What did this old man of yours say?"

Morwenna wanted to tell. She did. She thought talking might help her make some sense of it all. But no sooner did she decide to tell than a cold wind began to curl around her ears, a wind that whispered words:

Say not who you are or what you have
or before your time all shall be lost,
both you and they!

Morwenna was so startled by these words
from nowhere that, even as she wondered *whose*
voice it was, she instantly shut her mouth, afraid
to speak.

Miss Helga, thinking she simply hadn't heard
Morwenna answer, called, "What did he say?"

"I didn't tell you," Morwenna replied, still
trying to recall the voice.

Crossly now, Miss Helga demanded to know
about these wishes. But though Morwenna
wanted more than ever to explain, the voice had
frightened her too badly. Perhaps she could find
another way to talk about it. . . .

"An old man," she began, pausing to see if
the Voice would return. When it did not, she
went on. "An old man . . . right outside—"
Suddenly, Morwenna began to laugh. It all
seemed ridiculous. "An old man turned to dust,"
she exclaimed.

"Dust?" cried Miss Helga, confused as much
by Morwenna's sudden change of mood as by
her words.

Morwenna, giggling, nodded yes.

"Show me," the chamber maid insisted. Taking Morwenna by the hand, she pulled her out of the throne room into the hall. There lay the dust. Miss Helga studied it closely.

"Ordinary dust!" she announced and with a sweep of her cloth whisked it away.

In her heart Morwenna felt a cold, stabbing pain.

*M*ISS Helga bustled Morwenna back to work. She told the girl she must stop daydreaming if she wanted to keep her place, and reminded her how hard positions were to find. Then, softening, she began to tease, telling her that if she ever wanted to get home that night—it was Friday—she had better get busy.

The thought of going home to her mother lifted Morwenna's spirits. What was there to feel glum about?

What had happened—or what, she reminded herself, she *thought* had happened—was probably only what Miss Helga had called it: nonsense, a daydream.

Morwenna returned to polishing the king's throne. But as she worked, notions of home slipped away. Her mind drifted back to the old man, and to what she thought he had said, to his gnarled, tapping fingers.

As she puzzled about it all, as she slowly rubbed the smooth, glossy surface of the throne, the wood grew bright enough for her to see her own reflection. Morwenna blinked. Was that *her* face looking back?

The image was of an older woman.

Astonished, Morwenna stared at the face that stared at her. Gradually, it began to change, becoming her face, but as she had been when five years old. Then the image changed again, growing older one moment, younger the next, as if unsure what to be.

Upset, Morwenna quickly took her cloth and rubbed over the reflection. She decided she was being silly. It was just as Miss Helga said: the very notion that she had been given five wishes— why, it *was* laughable.

Still, as she laughed, she thought how much fun it would be to have wishes, for wishing sunny days, for games, endless jokes . . . Then it occurred to her: if, if that old man *had* given her five wishes, why then, why not use one? After all, if she made a wish, and that wish worked, she'd know for sure she did have wishes. If it didn't work, why then, *that* would be the end of that!

Morwenna glanced over the throne. Miss Helga was working hard on the far side of the room, paying no attention to her.

Kneeling down, eyes closed, Morwenna whispered, "I wish . . . I wish . . . I wish I were so rich I didn't have to work."

She waited. All she heard was Miss Helga's scolding words: "Morwenna! Stop this nonsense or I'll let you go! You're not a rich young lady! You must work!"

Morwenna sighed. Whatever that old man was, or said, no matter where he'd gone, or the tricks he'd played, it *was* only a joke. She was just as she had always been. She stood up. Somehow, she felt relieved.

By way of reassuring herself, she stole a quick glance at her reflection in the polished wood of the throne. There she was, herself at twelve, with a bright and merry face. Good, she thought.

I have no wishes. And after all, what does it matter?

She liked who she was.

And yet . . . and yet . . . nagging thoughts remained. Something had happened. But what?

II

*O*NCE Ruthvin and Sibald reached the main courtyard of the palace, they ordered every gate closed and every nearby citizen stopped. But the king saw no one who reminded him of the man with the wishes.

"To think I had him in my hands," he fumed, "him and his five wishes."

"And he's capable of doing great harm," added Sibald.

The king retired gloomily to a private room. "Sibald," he said, "do you think that the person I met might have disguised himself, completely changing his appearance?"

"Forgive me, Majesty," said Sibald, "you have no idea what he looked like to begin with."

King Ruthvin became furious. "He must be

somewhere!" he cried. "And when I catch him, he'll be hanged. That will show people what I think of anyone who puts himself above me." Raging, he sent Sibald to search throughout the city.

Sibald did as he was told, but met with no more success than when the palace had been searched. Empty-handed, he reported to the king.

"Fool!" Ruthvin shouted, and he ordered Sibald out of his sight. Then the king told a servant to get his coach and private guards ready. He would search the countryside himself.

"*D*ONE!" announced Miss Helga to Morwenna, as she gathered up her buckets and brooms. "Time to go!" But as they set out to leave the palace, they discovered all the gates were closed. No one was being allowed out. Morwenna had never known such a thing to happen.

"Nothing to worry about," the chamber maid assured her.

She led Morwenna down to the lowest kitchen in the palace, behind an old pantry. There, inside an unused closet, was a door. "A porter's entrance," Miss Helga explained with a wink. "Hasn't been used for years—except by me."

In moments, she and Morwenna were beyond the palace walls, making their way through crowds of people.

W HILE the palace was rich and splendid, the city was cluttered and reeked of decay. Restless crowds surged through narrow, filthy streets. Little sunlight reached the ground. People shouted. Donkeys brayed. Cart drivers called to clear the alleyways. Beggars, old and young, pleaded for alms. Morwenna was always glad to leave such scenes behind.

W HEN the girl journeyed back and forth between her home and the city, she didn't travel alone. She went with Swen, her special friend, a boy a little older than she. Quite alone in the world, he made his living driving a mule cart from the country to the city and back, hauling goods from the town where they both lived, where they had grown inseparable as friends. Every Sunday evening Swen brought Morwenna to the city. Every Friday night he took her home.

Morwenna spied Swen from a distance, waiting patiently as always. He was swapping jokes with everyone who passed by, occasionally flicking the hair out of his eyes with a smart shake of his head.

Oh Swen! Like a young prince he was, tall and strong for his age, with blond, thatched hair over a pleasant, always smiling face—not one mean thing about him. How much the opposite of Ruthvin.

The moment Swen saw Morwenna, he leaped on his cart, then onto the seat where he did a handstand, wagging his feet to make her laugh.

"My feet got tired waiting," he called as she approached. "Thought you'd never come."

"If I knew you were going to be so *hand* some," she retorted as she climbed into the cart, "I'd have been faster."

"The two of you," chided Miss Helga, refusing to laugh at Morwenna's joke. "Now, Swen," she said, "she's caught in a mood twixt this and that. A perfect fluff of confusion. Don't egg her on any more."

She turned to Morwenna, trying to look severe. "Early Monday morning, my dear. And if you want to keep your position, leave your fairy tales at home."

"What's the matter with her?" asked Swen once she had gone.

"Sometimes I think scolding is the only way she knows to speak," said Morwenna.

Swen gathered up the reins. "Ready to go?"

Morwenna, happy to be on her way, happy to be with Swen, gave a loud, laughing, "Yes."

*T*HEY had not gone very far into the countryside when Morwenna pulled a small piece of paper from her traveling bag.

"What's that?" Swen demanded with a groan. "Not lessons." Since he had never been to school, Morwenna took it upon herself to teach him now and then.

"Just a riddle," she told him. "You know I love them."

"But I never get the answers," Swen returned. "What's more, I don't think I ever will." He set his face into a look of mock sorrow. "I am what I am. I'll never be more."

"Of course you will," Morwenna insisted, hitting him playfully on the leg. "Anyway, I worked hard on this all week. You have to guess." Paying no attention to his protests, she read what she had written. "When bright, it's dark, when darkest, it's gone. When gone for good, so are you.— What am I?"

Swen struggled with the riddle, looking so intense that Morwenna couldn't keep from laughing.

"Give up?" she cried.

Swen shrugged, disconsolate.

"When bright, it's dark," she repeated, "when darkest, it's gone. When gone for good, so are you What am I? Why, silly, it's your shadow!"

"I never do get riddles, do I?" Swen said, upset and stung by both his failure and her laughter.

Morwenna's heart went out to him. "It's not important," she said. Leaning over, she kissed him on the cheek. Swen looked up, surprised, his good humor restored.

*T*HEY traveled a while before Swen, the reins easy in his hands, asked Morwenna if she had had a good week, if anything new had happened. Her heart sank at the question. Thoughts about what had occurred that afternoon returned, and with them, her sense of uncertainty. She wondered what Swen, with his straight-forward ways, would make of it. She decided to tell him. But at just that moment the Voice, that voice from a cold nowhere, began to cut about her ear:

> *Say not who you are or what you have*
> *or before your time all shall be lost,*
> *both you and they.*

Morwenna felt like crying out, "But *who* am I? *What* have I? *When* is my time? *What* shall be lost?" The Voice, however, made her feel she couldn't speak. Instead of answering Swen's question, she said only, "No, nothing happened to me. What about you?"

"Nothing new with me, either," he replied. "Which is fine. I like things the way they are."

W ITHOUT her understanding why, Morwenna's gloominess returned. She felt uncomfortable, ill at ease, unhappy with her private thoughts. But she remained silent, afraid to say anything that might bring back the Voice.

From time to time Swen glanced at her. "Something the matter?" he said finally. "Never saw you so serious. Not angry at me, are you?"

Morwenna tried to shake free of her mood. "Of course not," she told him, vexed with herself. "Why should I be?"

"Sometimes," said Swen, "I get the feeling I'm too simple for you. That's why."

Resolving once and for all to push her annoying thoughts away, Morwenna slipped an arm through Swen's. "I like you the way you are," she insisted, to reassure herself as much as him.

*T*HE sun began to set as they cut over hills, down through valleys. The light grew dim. The air cooled. Treetops trembled. Birds skimmed low, wheeling and darting gracefully.

A white mist rose from the dells, while far to the west the sky was swept with strokes of purple, orange and red.

Morwenna gazed at it in wonder. It was the most beautiful sunset she'd ever seen. "Lovely, isn't it?" she said in a whisper.

"Sure is," Swen replied, "best mule in the whole world."

His answer made Morwenna smile. He seldom noticed beautiful things. And when she looked again at the sunset, at the first stars, Morwenna felt sad. She wondered why.

Gradually, as she looked up, as she attempted to understand her troubled mood, Morwenna realized it was loneliness she felt. She had never sensed it before. Why now? she worried.

Without an answer, and wanting comfort,

Morwenna moved closer to Swen. No, she told herself, she didn't want things to change any more than he.

* * *

THEIR way was lit by a floating moon and the dancing light of fireflies. Magical, Morwenna thought. And thinking so made her feel bold.

"Swen," she said cautiously, afraid the cold Voice might make her stop again. "Swen, do you believe in magic?"

Swen snapped his head up from a doze and said, "What?"

"Magic," Morwenna repeated. "Do you belive in it?"

Swen considered. "Should I?" He yawned.

"It's *your* thought I want," she told him. "Do you believe?"

"Wishes, I mean," Morwenna tried. "What about them?"

Swen shrugged. "I never think about them one way or the other," he said.

"Don't you have any thoughts?" Morwenna

said, frustrated by the way he was ducking her questions.

"Ah, Morwenna," Swen said with another yawn. "You're too deep for me. No more riddles. Not tonight. I wouldn't know magic or wishes if they sat right down next to me."

Swen had hardly spoken when a great clattering came from behind them. Trumpets blared. Hoofbeats rattled. Morwenna turned and saw torches.

"Make way for the king! The king must pass!"

The next instant, a troop of soldiers on galloping horses burst from the dark. A coach came hard behind.

As the horses drew closer, too close, Swen tried turning his cart to one side of the road. The coach swept past. As it did, one of its rear wheels struck the cart, causing a violent jolt which sent Morwenna flying into the air.

Twisting frantically to right herself, she suddenly saw faces all about, faces exploding from the dark—wailing, crying, calling her name. There were hands too, hands of gossamer white, hands which reached out as if to help her.

At the same moment, Swen, who had recovered from the shock, saw Morwenna's danger. He leaped from the cart and tried to catch her. But he reached her only as she touched the ground.

For Morwenna saved herself, flipping over—a somersault—to come safely down on her own two feet. Though unhurt, she was stunned by the vision of faces and the reaching hands. She gazed about in wonder, looking for them. But they had vanished.

Only Swen was there.

"Are you hurt?" he cried, standing close, greatly concerned. "Did I get you quick enough? Are you all right?"

Turning to him, Morwenna realized that he thought that he—not she herself—had saved her from the fall.

"I'm fine," she told him. "Not hurt at all." Gently, she pushed away his hands and climbed back into the cart. It had not been seriously damaged.

Swen stood where he was, looking at her. "Morwenna," he said, "you were almost killed."

"I'm fine," she assured him.

"But I saved you."

Morwenna didn't answer. She had begun thinking furiously about what she had seen. Who were those people? What were they? Why should there have been *anything*?

Swen, meanwhile, waited for her to say more. "Lucky I'm so fast, isn't it? he asked.

Her mind in a whirl, not knowing what to say, Morwenna looked at him. "Thank you," was all she managed.

Swen studied her, puzzled, then pulled himself into the cart and took up the reins. "No," he said with a shake of his head, "you don't know how lucky you are. You near broke your neck."

What Morwenna did know was that she didn't want to talk. She needed to think. She understood that she had been in great danger. She knew, too, that she had saved herself. Swen had nothing to do with it. But most of all there had been visions, visions of spirits, spirits who had called her name . . .

S WEN glanced at Morwenna from time to time as they moved along, trying to understand what was on her mind, why she kept so silent. If she had saved him, *he* would have said something. He knew he would.

At last he said, "Glad you didn't get hurt."

"I'm glad, too," Morwenna replied off-handedly.

"Saving you was, well, easy for me," Swen said. "Natural—we being such good friends and all. But you're not saying much about anything. I wish you would."

Morwenna, pulled from her thoughts, didn't know what to answer. How could she explain, without explaining everything? And if she did, wouldn't the Voice come back? She didn't want that.

"Did you hear me?" Swen asked, softer now.

Morwenna's thoughts were so removed that for a brief moment she felt he was a stranger. She had to remind herself that this was Swen, Swen her closest friend, Swen whom she'd known all her life. But still, she didn't want to talk. Not to him. Not to anyone. And that upset her. To hide her confusion, she took the easy way. She pretended she hadn't heard him correctly.

"I know it's late," she said. "But we'll get home all right."

Swen wanted to object, to say she wasn't being fair. Instead he began to think it was he. He must have done something wrong. But what?

For the rest of the ride neither spoke a word.

III

BY the time they reached Morwenna's home it was very late. No lanterns shone. She climbed down from the wagon, then hurried inside.

"Good night!" Swen called as he watched her disappear. He wished she would say or do something to reassure him. Left alone, he felt like crying, shouting, striking out. They had always been such good friends. What had happened?

After one last look, and still wondering what it was that he had done to make her so unfriendly, he started off. But he felt too miserable to go to his own empty hut.

Instead, he went to the inn. There, he knew, he'd find company.

*I*NSIDE Morwenna's house it was dark and still. Her mother was already asleep. But as Morwenna stood in the silence she became aware of the small cottage as never before. Its smell. Its warmth. Its intense, close familiarity. The sensation was almost overpowering, suffocating.

Then she remembered she hadn't said her thanks to Swen, something she always did. She hurried out to look for him. But he was gone.

For a moment she gazed up into the sky. She had never seen so many stars.

*W*HEN Swen arrived at the inn he found it crowded with people. He had thought he wanted company, but once he saw people joking and laughing, his gloom doubled. He took himself into a corner and sat down alone. It was there the inn keeper found him.

"How's my boy tonight?" he called, with a

friendly slap on Swen's back. "Don't you want anyone to see you?"

Swen, hardly looking up, shook his head. "I'm pretty tired," he said.

The inn keeper studied him. "Are you sure that's all?"

"Yes," said Swen, glumly.

For a moment the inn keeper gazed at the boy. Then he sat down. "It's that friend of yours, isn't it?" he said. "Morwenna."

Swen shook his head again.

"It's not for me to give advice," the inn keeper said, leaning closer. "Not about your friends. But you're all alone in the world. I'll speak to you like a father.

"Now, Swen," he began, "what am I? An inn keeper. And what are you? A mule driver. Look around. There's our carpenter. And one of our farmers . . . So it goes. The same as you and me. Ah, Swen, your friend, Morwenna, she's too fine for you."

"I don't want to hear," cried Swen.

"I know you've been best friends but, Swen, you're getting to an age when you have to see things the way they are. People like you and me, there's no fancy in us. True friends appreciate you for what you are. Now, friend to friend, how about some supper. On the house."

Swen stared into his hands. "I wish I could be different!"

"Do you now?" said the inn keeper with a smile. "I can see it. The boy mule driver who becomes grand adviser to the king. Better yet, king himself. Lord knows, we couldn't do worse than what we've got. Come on, boy, food always does you good."

"I don't want to eat," Swen sulked, thinking he was being made sport of.

Now it was the inn keeper who felt offended. "Isn't my food good enough?" he asked.

Swen got up. "I'd rather be alone," he said, and started toward the door.

Feeling his friendship rejected, and by a sullen boy at that, the inn keeper called, "Well, maybe you are a fool. You'll not be changed from that."

Swen spun about, enraged at the taunt. He wanted to say or do something to regain his dignity. But when he could think of nothing, he felt even more miserable. Hiding his shame, he rushed from the inn, and went home to bed.

As for the inn keeper, he turned from the door, just as angry.

*T*HAT same night King Ruthvin was racing down country roads in search of the man who had offered him the wishes. Though his carriage almost collided with a cart on the road, the king pushed on. But he found no one who fitted his vague description.

At the fifth inn, the owner, a woman, was brought forward.

Leaning from his carriage window, Ruthvin asked if she were loyal to her king.

"I hope so," said the frightened woman.

"Then listen to me carefully," Ruthvin said. "I am looking for a man, someone who came from the city just today. Strange, secretive perhaps. Perhaps he pretended to have magic. Did anyone of that sort come by today?"

With great relief the owner was able to say an honest, "No."

King Ruthvin then told her that if such a person did stop and she reported the fact, it would be worth her while. But, he warned, if she did see such a man, and failed to report it, she would suffer pain. "Do I make myself clear?" he asked.

The woman managed a nervous yes, and the king called his coach driver to hurry on.

*I*T was almost midnight when King Ruthvin reached the inn in the town where Swen and Morwenna lived. Despite the late hour, he roused the same inn keeper who had spoken with Swen earlier that evening.

When the man appeared, King Ruthvin leaned from his carriage window and asked the questions he had asked since he set out: had he seen any unusual sort of a man that day?

The inn keeper was still angry over his exchange with Swen. The young fellow wanted to be different than he is, he told himself. Very well, I'll show him what being different means. I'll teach him a lesson he won't forget.

The inn keeper told the king about Swen. "He's only a boy, Your Majesty," he explained, "but he came from the city today. And that's exactly what he said to me; he wanted to be different than he was. Maybe he's your man."

King Ruthvin considered. He considered the time, and his fierce desire to punish someone quickly so as to set an example.

"How old is this person?" he demanded.

"Fourteen or so."

"What about his parents?"

"Died long ago."

Again the king considered. This boy might prove to be an easy scapegoat. Who would care? What did one boy matter more or less?

At once Ruthvin ordered the inn keeper to give him directions for finding Swen.

"He won't come to any harm, will he?" the inn keeper asked, suddenly uneasy about what he had done.

"Nothing for you to worry about," snapped the king.

S URROUNDED by soldiers, King Ruthvin was led to the small wooden hut where Swen lived alone. One soldier beat upon the door.

"Who's there?" came Swen's sleepy voice.

"Friends," returned Ruthvin, as his men drew their swords.

Swen stepped out. Instantly, two soldiers jumped forward and took him by the arms.

"You are under arrest," the king announced.

"But what have I done?" asked Swen, completely surprised.

"You hold dangerous magic," said the king, trying to keep from smiling. "And holding magic without my permission is an act of treason punishable by death."

"But Your Majesty, believe me, I don't have magic," Swen protested. "At least, I don't think I do."

"Do you wish to confess?" asked the king, ignoring Swen's words.

"To what?"

"To being a wizard."

"Forgive me, Your Majesty," Swen said, "I don't know anything about that."

The king smiled scornfully. "Next you'll tell me you don't have wishes."

"Wishes?" cried Swen, astounded.

"Admit it or not, you trouble my realm," said Ruthvin, becoming bored with the charade of taking the boy seriously. All he wanted to do was publicly pronounce Swen the Wizard, then hang him to show his determination to resist all who would challenge his rule.

"Please, sir," Swen said, "are you sure?"

"Do you dare question me?" cried the king. "Take him away!"

As Swen was marched off, his first thought was that the king would quickly realize his mistake and let him go. But as he went an idea came into his head: if Morwenna were to hear that he, Swen, had been thought to be some wizard, might she not pay better attention to him? The idea pleased him greatly. And the more he thought about it, the more Swen hoped that the king's mistake would show other people as well that he was not considered a fool by everyone.

WHEN Morwenna woke the next morning she lay in bed a while looking about her small, but bright, room. It was filled with things she loved, treasures she had saved to remind her of what she'd been and done.

43

As long as she could recall, this room had been hers. But that morning she couldn't help feeling it was cramped, cluttered, uncomfortable.

She didn't want to see it so, and tried to drop back to sleep. Instead, all that had happened the day before filled her mind. Determined to push it from her thoughts, she got up and began to dress.

But standing in front of her mirror, brushing her long hair as she'd done countless times, Morenna suddenly saw a man's face in the mirror behind her own. She whirled around. No one was there. She turned back to the mirror. Not only was the man's face gone, her own reflection had vanished as well.

Trembling, Morwenna sat down on the edge of her bed, then she peeked at the mirror. Her own face had reappeared, like a moon coming out from behind clouds. For the first time she allowed herself the fullness of her fear. *Everything seemed to be changing.* More than ever, she felt the need to talk to someone.

The person Morwenna had always talked to, the one she loved most, who could always comfort her, was her mother.

MORWENNA finished dressing and hurried to the meadow. There, in early morning, it was always warm, and there her mother had her garden. Morwenna knew she'd already be hard at work.

As Morwenna went down the hill she could see her mother working at the earth. Her gray braided hair, which made her look old and young at the same time, hung over one shoulder. When she heard Morwenna's call she looked up.

Their eyes met. Again, just as in her room, Morwenna felt like a stranger, even shy. She tried to smile. It wouldn't come. Instead, she threw herself into her mother's arms, wanting more than anything to tell her all that had happened, her feelings, her fears. She found she could not. As the words formed in her mind, the warning Voice spoke again with clipped, cold precision:

*Say not who you are or what you have
or all shall be lost, both you and they.*

On the point of tears, Morwenna hugged her mother hard. They sat down on the ground face

45

to face. "Mama," she began, "do you believe in magic?"

Morwenna's mother stroked her hair and looked at her for a long time. "When we were young," she said, "I did. So did others. We believed there was a person who kept all the wishes in the land."

"Only one?" Morwenna asked.

Her mother nodded. "The Wizard."

Morwenna had never known of such a person before. Yet when she heard of him—even though the sun was warm—she felt a coldness inside her, a shadow.

"What happened to this . . . wizard?" she asked.

"I don't know," her mother replied. "We believed he lived for many years. But no one knew if he were alive or dead. Some thought one way, some the other. There were even those who searched for him. Oh, how people wanted him to return! How needed he was . . . and is. We also believed that he wouldn't die before passing on the wishes to someone. We all hoped we would be the one."

"Mama," asked Morwenna, "do you still believe in that wizard?"

"I would like to."

"Why?"

"Magic," her mother said, "is a kind of hope. And wishes are like dreams. When we have them, we can make things change. Without, we stay the same."

Morwenna noticed that while her mother spoke she averted her eyes. "Why won't you look at me?" she asked.

Her mother shook her head. "I don't know," she said, turning back.

One look into her eyes and Morwenna felt older than her mother, felt she had more answers, felt as if her mother was asking *her* for help. It shocked her.

"Mama," she whispered, deeply moved, "something has happened. I don't know what it is."

At the top of the hill a man appeared. "It's the king!" he cried. "Here, in town. They say he's caught the Wizard. Brought him to the square!"

At the words, Morwenna felt a flood of joy, aware suddenly that if it were true—if there were someone who was the Wizard—she would be much happier.

Greatly excited, she began to run up the hill. "Morwenna!" her mother called after her. Morwenna was in too much of a hurry to stop.

IV

THERE was a great crowd of people in the town square. Morwenna could not see over their heads, but at the rear of the throng she found an abandoned wagon, horses still in harness. Once on the wagon she could see everything.

A line of soldiers kept the crowd from reaching a gallows that had been set up at the far end of the square. Not far from the platform, also protected by soldiers, was the royal carriage. Inside, King Ruthvin sat and watched.

Morwenna understood well enough what was happening: someone was about to be hanged.

The people in the square were shouting, demanding that the gallows be torn down. They had seen hangings before, all at the king's command. Twice Morwenna thought the crowd would break through the soldiers' line. Each time the soldiers drove them back.

Then more soldiers appeared, escorting someone from behind the carriage. Morwenna looked to see who it was. To her astonishment she saw that it was Swen, his hands tightly bound.

THE moment they saw Swen, the crowd began to shout, "Free him! Free him! He's just a boy!"

Their cries made no difference. Swen was led to the gallows platform, where a soldier fitted the noose around his neck.

Morwenna could hardly breathe.

Two soldiers stepped forward. One beat a drum, the other unrolled a scroll. In a voice that carried over the crowd, the second soldier began to read.

"Swen," he read, "you are accused of high treason against the rightful rule of King Ruthvin. You have refused to give up your magic to your king. You have claimed to be the Wizard."

A murmur ran through the crowd. Morwenna, meanwhile, watched and listened with increasing horror.

"Therefore," the soldier continued, "King Ruthvin condemns you to be hanged until you are dead. Let this be a warning to all who stand against him. So shall all his enemies perish. Long live King Ruthvin!"

Turning, the soldier asked Swen if he had any last words.

SWEN looked up. As if to beg, he held out his bound hands. Morwenna began to cry. Her dearest friend, condemned by his king.

The crowd grew still.

"I don't know what to say," Swen began, speaking slowly, miserably, not sure what words to use. "I don't know why I'm here. I thought it was a mistake. I never knew I was a wizard. At least, I didn't know till now. But then, I never was so good at figuring things. Maybe I'm what they say. I'm glad I'm someone.

"If I have wishes," continued Swen, stepping forward, "and I hope I do, I'd wish that some-

one—I won't say her name—would come to see
me. And then," he cried, "I'd wish that no matter who or what or why I am . . . I'd wish I
could stay alive!"

The soldiers rudely shoved Swen back and
stood him over the gallows trap. The drummer
beat his drum again. The hangman made ready.
The crowd screamed in rage.

Morwenna was speechless with anguish. How
could anyone be so horrible as to hurt poor and
harmless Swen, he, who had never, ever, done
one thing wrong? Knowing perfectly well that
she was the "someone" Swen had spoken of,
she tried, with all her heart, to think of some
way to help him.

Yet even as she watched, sickened by the
sight, the two soldiers stepped aside to let the
hangman do his task. It was too much for
Morwenna. She paid no mind to the cold winds
which were now whirling around her head,
crying:

Use them well! Waste them not!

Without thinking, Morwenna whispered,
"Oh, I wish that Swen would go free!"

What happened next, happened very quickly.

*N*o sooner did Morwenna speak, than out of the sky a great bird plummeted, filling the air with one long wondrous, wailing note. Its feathers were green, its beak golden, its eyes black, its blue talons long and sharp.

Like an arrow, the bird dove straight to the gallows. With one of its wings, it split the hanging rope in two. Turning completely about, it plucked the noose away with its talons. Then with a slash of its beak, it cut apart the ropes that bound Swen's hands together.

Just as quickly the bird flew aloft. And just as quickly, it disappeared.

*S*WEN was the first to realize he was free. One long leap took him from the gallows. Two more strides and he was past the soldiers. Another took him to the middle of the crowd.

Frantically, he shoved people aside. Others
fled, screaming.

From his carriage King Ruthvin cried: "Catch
that man! A thousand coins to catch that man!"

The soldiers surged forward. The crowd
fought them back. Swen, meanwhile, zig-
zagged through the square, looking for escape.

"Swen!" cried Morwenna, standing on the
wagon's seat. "Here!"

Swen turned. Morwenna waved her arms. He
saw her, raced for the wagon and jumped in.
The second he did, Morwenna, who had been
holding the reins, shouted to the horses. They
galloped away while Swen, lying in the bottom
of the wagon, struggled to catch his breath.

Morwenna's head was all but bursting. She
could hardly think. "Did I do that?" she kept
asking herself. "Was it me who set him free?
Impossible!" she felt like crying out. That was
magic!

*A*s soon as Swen could breathe again, he
crawled up front to where Morwenna
was doing her best to control the horses. He

called for their reins. She handed them over, hoping that with his driver's skill, he would bring the frantic horses to a stop. But as soon as Swen took control, he only urged them to go on faster.

They never slowed, not even when Swen took a sweeping turn that nearly tumbled the wagon. He had taken a dirt road that led into the Great Forest.

*A*FTER an hour of furious driving, Swen let out a long, low, whistling sigh of relief and pulled the horses to a halt. With a shake of his head, he closed his eyes and wiped the sweat from his face. "Morwenna," he began, speaking in hushed tones, "did you hear what they said about me? *Magic . . .*" He was almost afraid to say the word.

Morwenna watched him intently.

"They say," he continued, "that I have magic. And Morwenna . . . *honest* . . . I didn't think I had. Ever. But then, I made a wish. No, two wishes! First I wished you'd come. And . . . you did. Then I wished myself to stay alive. That worked, too. *Both of them!*

"And that bird . . . I never saw anything like it before." He glanced at her shyly. "I think I have . . . magic, Morwenna. I must."

She didn't know what to say. It had been magic. That she knew. But was it Swen's magic as he believed or . . . hers?

"Morwenna," Swen said, hurrying on, "you know me better than anyone. I'm not very important. I know that. Guess everybody knows. But last night when the king—the *king* himself, Morwenna—came to my house . . ." He shook his head with the wonder of it. "Kind of an honor, you know. Even if it is from him. He said that . . . I . . . me . . . I was the Wizard. Guess you know all about him. I never did. Just think of it . . . Me . . . a wizard . . ." He stared into his hands.

"Are you?" asked Morwenna.

Swen turned to look at her. "Would you like that?"

"Yes," she replied.

"Would it be good enough?"

"Good enough for what?"

"For you. For everyone. I mean, people don't think much of me. They don't. You don't."

Morwenna pressed him once again. "Swen," she said, "are you the Wizard?"

After a moment he answered, "I'm not sure. All I know is, they said I did have magic . . . wishes . . . And when I used them . . . the wishes, that is . . . they worked." He peered around to make sure no one heard him.

"Where are we?" asked Morwenna.

"Beginning of the Great Forest," Swen replied, picking up the reins. "And we'd better get past the beginning. They'll be coming. Ruthvin won't give up. I know he won't." Without another word, he flicked the reins. Once more they moved beneath the trees.

Needing to put her thoughts together, trying to understand, Morwenna crawled to the back of the wagon. From there she watched the road they traveled roll out like an unwinding spool of thread.

K ING Ruthvin had seen it all. He had watched Swen being led to the gallows. He had listened to the accusation which he himself composed. And, as Swen spoke his first words, he had smiled in satisfaction.

But hearing the boy speak of wishes had made

Ruthvin hold his breath. When after a few seconds nothing happened, he relaxed. Then the bird appeared! Ruthvin had watched as Swen, set free, jumped from the gallows, cut through the crowd, leaped upon a wagon and raced from the square.

The king was stunned. It was all perfectly clear what Swen's escape meant. Along with everyone else Ruthvin had heard it. Swen had wished himself free. Swen was the Wizard.

The danger to his kingdom was clear to Ruthvin. The news of Swen's escape would spread quickly, make people restless.

No matter what the cost, the king knew he must track the Wizard down. Twice he had had him in his grasp. Twice he had gone free.

The more he thought, the more certain he became that the only one he could trust to catch the Wizard was himself. Everybody else would be too frightened.

He would pursue the Wizard. And when he found him, he would destroy him utterly.

Within the hour, King Ruthvin had disguised himself as a beggar, hidden a dagger in his clothing and set off after Swen.

*S*WEN drove deeper and deeper into the forest until the road became little more than a path. He climbed down from the wagon. The horses could pull it no further.

"Where are we?" asked Morwenna.

"Not far enough," Swen returned. "I don't want them to get even close to me."

Morwenna watched silently as he began unhitching the two horses. Then she said, "And me?"

Swen stopped his work to look at her. She was still sitting on the wagon. For the first time since his escape, he smiled. "Don't worry," he said. "I wasn't going to leave you. Never have, have I?" He climbed up on one of the horses. "Come on," he said, pointing to the other. "Can't waste more time."

Morwenna studied his face. Perhaps, she told herself, it *was* he who had saved her on the road the night before, brought her to the square, saved himself. Maybe it wasn't her at all . . .

She climbed on the other horse.

Swen gave her a big smile. "All you have to do is follow."

THE forest grew darker. Moss hung like the beards of old men. Vines, as if they were roots from the sky, brushed Morwenna's face. Endless fields of ferns covered the ground. Here and there golden bars of sunlight touched the forest floor. Where they did, bunches of flowers grew, rainbows springing from the earth.

Morwenna began to see things that didn't seem real, like faces of old people peeking from behind the ferns. They seemed to be following her. She wanted Swen to ride faster, to leave the faces far behind. He only plodded on. "Slow and steady," he told her. "Slow and steady."

Once, Morwenna was sure she saw an old man gliding through the trees, floating above the ground. His thin white hair and tattered clothing fluttered in the air. Was he calling her name? "Swen!" she cried. "Look!" She pointed toward the man who hovered in midair, looking at her.

"What's the matter?" said Swen.

"There," Morwenna said. "Don't you see him? He's right there!"

Swen looked where Morwenna pointed, but only shook his head. "Nothing but trees. Come on, we're wasting time."

Morwenna looked again. The old man was gone. Dreading the thought of being left behind, she spurred her horse to catch up.

*I*T wasn't long before she began hearing sounds. At first she wasn't sure what they were. Soon enough she knew. They were voices, chanting softly. Soon she understood their words: her name, endlessly repeated.

Then she heard bright laughter, familiar laughter. Her own, she realized. Again and again it came, before seeming to drift away. Soon it, too, was gone. She started to say something to Swen, but he was so intent upon the trail, his back to her, that she didn't dare.

Finally, visions came. Her mind seemed to make patterns of the trees, the leaves, the flowers and the ferns. But gradually, the patterns grew in clarity. They became scenes of herself—playing, dancing, laughing—when she was young. Other scenes showed her older, and the last vision was of Morwenna walking from the throne room just the day before. She had seen her entire past. But nothing of a future.

She trembled.

*A*LL that day they traveled. Only when it became too dark to see did Swen halt the horses. They had reached a small clearing, a patch of grass surrounded by towering trees. Morwenna felt as if no one had ever come to it before.

Swen tied the horses to a bush, then sat down against one of the great tree trunks. "Plenty of room for you," he said, with a yawn, offering her a spot nearby.

Morwenna shook her head. She didn't feel the least bit tired.

Almost immediately, Swen's eyes began to close. "I sure hope I've got the magic," he said.

"Why?" Morwenna asked.

"People," he said sleepily, "people would think more of me. Yes . . . I think . . . they . . .

would." His eyes closed. His chest heaved. He was asleep.

Without a sound the horses slipped their halters and trotted noiselessly into the woods. Morwenna jumped to catch them, but they were quickly gone. She didn't dare follow.

She huddled down opposite Swen and waited, her heart beating faster and faster. Whatever was going to happen, was about to begin.

*O*NE by one the icy pointed stars blinked out. Yet Morwenna could see in the absolute blackness—not with her eyes, but with her very being.

Gradually, the forest came alive. Eyes, watching eyes, bloomed here, there, only to fade away. Morwenna heard footsteps, too, as if someone were walking up and down a great hallway. Doors opened and shut. Someone was trying to find a way out.

Morwenna asked herself: is that me?

*S*HE heard—but did not feel—a rising, falling wind. Then faces appeared, faces bursting suddenly into view, flaming, fading, leaving holes in the dark.

One face remained. Morwenna recognized it— the face of the man she had seen over her shoulder in the mirror that morning. The one who had followed her in the woods. The ancient man she had met outside the throne room doors. The one who said he was giving her the wishes. The one who had turned to dust. *Pindel.* There he was again, glowing, his white face throbbing.

Morwenna covered her eyes with her hands, but she felt them pulled away. She was forced to look. The old man was talking. She heard no words.

More faces appeared. All of them were old— ancient. Then came hands, hands that prayed, that reached out toward her. They were the hands she had seen the night before when she was thrown from the wagon.

How Morwenna knew she couldn't say, but as she looked she understood that the hands and faces belonged to wizards from times long gone.

Now they looked joyful. Now in sorrow. Now joyful again. It was as if each emotion reminded itself of what it was not, and rushed to become its opposite. Morwenna shut her eyes.

She heard the Voice.

Say not who you are or what you have
or before your time all shall be lost,
both you and they. Use them well.
Waste them not. Waste them not at all . . .

"Who are you?" Morwenna called out.

You know! You know!

"I don't!" she returned pressing her hands to her ears. Still she heard:

Leave, Morwenna! Hide the wishes!
Keep them safe! Protect them. Protect them!

"I don't have the wishes!" Morwenna cried. "I don't!"

You do! You saved Swen!

"He saved himself!"

You did!

"How could I?" pleaded Morwenna.

The wishes! The wishes!

"I don't know anything about the wishes!"

You shall learn! You shall learn!

"I'm not the Wizard! I'm not."

You are! You are! You are!

As the Voice echoed in her, around her, Morwenna felt overwhelmed. "Swen!" she screamed.

Instantly, Swen was awake. "Where are you?" he called.

"Here," Morwenna said, weak and in tears.

Swen came to her and put an arm around her shoulder. "What happened?" he asked.

Morwenna listened. There wasn't a sound. She looked. Nothing to see but stars. How could she explain? "The horses are gone," she said lamely.

"Don't worry. We'll get on. We always do. Oh, Morwenna, such wonderful dreams," he said, yawning. "Such magic . . . such wishes . . ." He fell asleep by her side.

Morwenna wanted nothing better than to sleep herself. It would not come. She felt only the great weight of the dark and silent night.

In that silence, in that dark, lurked the truth she couldn't deny. She, Morwenna, was the Wizard.

She.

V

D AWN. The damp ground steamed.
Trees and bushes bent under the
weight of dew. Morwenna, who had not slept,
shivered in the chill. I am the Wizard, she repeated to herself, trying to grasp the meaning.

Swen, across the way, remained asleep. His
breathing came softly. There was a smile on his
lips. How young he looks, thought Morwenna.

But gazing at him, she began to feel something new . . . pride that a wish of hers had
saved him from death. She had done that. She
held the gift of life.

A growing sense of what that meant, the
hugeness of the idea, came like a fountain to fill
her. Oh, what she might do, be and have! Before the day of the old man, it was as if she'd

lived in a small, dark room, which she needed permission to leave. Now she felt let loose in the universe. Carried by the wishes, she could go anywhere. Everything was in her reach.

How much she wanted to tell someone what had happened, what she had become! Swen, her closest friend should be the one.

Then Morwenna remembered. The Voice had taught her she wasn't allowed to say who she was. She didn't know what would happen if she did tell, but it would be fearsome. She had to find another way to let him know.

In seconds, Morwenna had another plan. As soon as Swen awoke, she would grant him anything he wanted. When he saw her make the wish that brought him his desire, he'd see that *she* had the wishes, not he.

What—she wondered—would he want? A castle, perhaps. A cloak of invisibility. A horse with wings. New worlds. Something. *Anything*. She could wish it all! And how happy Swen would be when he realized it was she who had the powers. She felt like laughing, dancing, leaping with joy. She nearly cried out to wake him. But in an instant she felt the cold wind wrap around her, heard the angry Voice:

Waste them not! Waste them not!

"The wishes are mine," Morwenna whispered fiercely. "I'll use them as I want."

Instantly, the winds softened, moaned.

Use them well. Use them well . . .

Morwenna shook her head. No one would tell her how to act; no one. If she wanted, she would use each and every wish as she chose.

A T last Swen woke. He stretched. He yawned. He pawed sleep from his eyes. He smiled at Morwenna, wiggling his toes to show he was awake.

"Good morning!" Morwenna called, hardly able to keep still in her excitement.

Swen stretched again, lifting his hands above his head. "Morwenna," he said. "I'm going to like being a wizard."

Morwenna laughed, thinking what fun it would be when he discovered the truth. "Do you really think you are?"

Swen grinned broadly. "Don't have much

choice, do I? I mean, I made those wishes before. Only figures I can do it again."

Morwenna was unable to hold back any longer. "What would you like to wish for most?" she asked.

Swen laughed now. "Guess I spent most of the night dreaming about that," he admitted.

Morwenna clapped her hands. "What did you decide?" she asked, then held her breath.

As if his ideas were too huge to see with open eyes, Swen closed his, leaned back against the tree, took a deep breath and said, "I'd wish for . . . breakfast."

"*Breakfast?*" echoed Morwenna, thinking perhaps she hadn't heard right.

"Sure. Breakfast. You forget? I never ate yesterday."

Morwenna felt she had walked down a flight of steps and stepped off—only to find the floor wasn't there. Her joy tumbled; she felt chilled. How could she wish for something as small as . . . breakfast . . . with something so huge as a wish?

"Then wish for it," she prompted, hoping suddenly that when he tried and failed, he'd see the truth.

Swen became embarrassed. "I tried," he said. "I don't think I've got it down right. The wishes won't work. I keep trying to remember how I made them before. Do you think my hands were a certain way . . .?" He made some fumbling efforts with his fingers. When nothing happened, he laughed sheepishly.

"Doesn't matter," he went on. "I think we'll be safe here. Enough wood to build a dozen houses. We can stay for years."

"Years!" Morwenna cried. He was drifting further away from the truth.

"Look here, Morwenna," Swen said earnestly, "next time they catch me, soon as they get close"—he made the motion of a dagger thrust—"I'll be finished. No, it's the forest for us."

"Swen," she said, "I don't want to stay."

For the first time that morning Swen really noticed her. "You don't?" he said, surprised.

Morwenna shook her head.

Frowning, Swen got up, shoved his hands into his pockets, looked around, started to whistle, stopped, then faced Morwenna. "All right, I'll take you where you want to go. At least till we find someone. Or a road that'll lead you out of the forest. That good enough?"

"Thank you," Morwenna said, aware that Swen was puzzled. She longed to explain. And though she felt grateful he wasn't going to abandon her, she felt guilty about accepting his company when he didn't know the truth.

Swen was still looking at her oddly. "Sure wish you'd be yourself again."

Morwenna averted her eyes. It was hard enough not being able to tell him what she wanted. It was harder pretending nothing was wrong. The truth was that Swen, her closest friend, had disappointed her. She felt ashamed to have the thought.

Morwenna sighed. It was only morning and already she felt exhausted. She had so many feelings. They all seemed to contradict.

With Swen in the lead, they started off.

*M*ORWENNA didn't feel hungry. She didn't know why, but simply accepted it. Swen, however, was starved. He reminded her again and again that he hadn't eaten. He wished for bread, an apple, even a forest stream to drink from. But no wish worked.

"Do you think maybe it's crossing my eyes that does it?" Swen asked once.

Before she could stop herself, Morwenna snapped, "Don't always be so stupid!"

With hurt surprise, Swen turned away. For the moment Morwenna didn't even care.

THE farther they traveled in the dark forest the more it became clear to Morwenna that Swen had no idea where he was going. At last, too tired to take another step, they stopped to rest in a clearing.

While Swen sprawled on the ground, Morwenna lay on her stomach, chin in her hands. She was certain they had come to a place they'd been before, certain they'd been marching around in circles.

"Morwenna," Swen said, turning toward her, "remember how you asked me what else I'd like to do with my wishes? Well, I've thought up other things."

She brushed the hair from her hot face. Perhaps he would wish for something new . . .

something important . . . so she could show her powers. "What are they?" she asked, her expectations rising.

Swen looped a finger through a hole in his shirt. "For a start," he said, "something new to wear. And a better wagon. I could earn more with a bigger one. And a blanket for my mule. Sometimes she gets awful cold and damp." He looked at Morwenna. "Any better?" he asked.

"Is that all you can think of?" Morwenna sighed, discouraged again.

Swen answered seriously. "I've got everything else."

"Is that what magic's for?" Morwenna heard herself demanding. "Things like that?"

Swen bolted up, tossing the hair from his face. "Come on, Morwenna. If you had the magic, you'd see. It's not so easy thinking up things."

"I wish I were alone!" Morwenna cried in frustration.

"I'm doing the best I can," returned Swen, hurt by her words. "I am!"

But Morwenna wasn't listening. She realized what she'd done; she had made a wish. Heart hammering, feeling frightened, she waited for it to work. But nothing happened.

"Anyway," said Swen, "you don't have the wishes. I do."

Morwenna frowned. Why hadn't the wish worked? Before she could think about it, seven men stepped from the forest. Each one held a sword.

THE moment the seven appeared, Morwenna and Swen jumped up, ready to run or defend themselves. But the strangers weren't there to fight. Instead, they stood their ground, as if reluctant to come closer. Dressed in rags, with feet bare, they seemed hesitant, almost shy. Their eyes were all on Swen.

"What do you want?" Morwenna asked.

One of the newcomers pointed nervously toward Swen. "Him," he said.

"Are you from the king?" Swen wanted to know. He had snatched a branch from the ground and was holding it up, ready to fight.

"Not us," another answered quickly. "We're his enemies."

"Then what do you want with me?" asked Swen, puzzled.

"Please, sir," said another, lowering his sword. "You're the Wizard."

Swen was startled. "How'd you know that?"

"Everybody knows."

"They do?" Swen said, pleased, and stealing a look at Morwenna.

"The king caught you," said yet another, "and was going to hang you. But you freed yourself."

"With a wish," called one of the others.

"And escaped," someone else added. "No one before has been able to do that. Then you came to the forest. That's when we discovered you. Please, we were told to bring you with us. We don't want to use force. Will you come now?"

Swen tried to grasp what was being said. "But why?" he asked again. "What can I do for you?"

"It will be explained," was the answer. "Will you come?"

Swen beckoned Morwenna to one side. "What do you think?" he whispered. "They look all right to me. And they might lead us to a road. Or some food."

Morwenna looked over her shoulder at the armed strangers. Part of her wanted Swen to go alone, to leave her. But when she glanced about at the forest and thought how far they had come, first by wagon, then horseback, then walking, when she considered what it might be like to be left alone with just the spirits and the Voice, her courage faltered. "I'll go," she said.

*T*HEY set off in a single line.

As she walked Morwenna brooded over her wish to be alone, made just before the strangers came. Why, she wondered, hadn't it worked? She knew she had the wishes, that she was the Wizard. Didn't the Voice say so?

The more she thought, the more she saw there must be rules about the wishes which she didn't understand. Some wishes worked. Others didn't. And she remembered that when the old man had given them to her, he spoke things she didn't clearly hear. Had he been trying to tell her the rules? How sorry she was not to have listened more closely . . .

There was the wish she'd made in the throne room, when she asked for riches. That hadn't worked. But the one freeing Swen from the gallows had.

Why?

The only rule she understood was that she could tell no one she was the Wizard, that the wishes were hers.

Then—with a start—she thought of something she hadn't considered: the old man in the palace had given her five wishes exactly. To save Swen she had used one. Only four wishes were left.

Only four, she realized.

A sudden sense of where she was, of how her situation had changed, came over her. There was Swen, walking in front, cheerful as usual. There were the seven men, moving steadily, guarding them, swords in hand. The forest was vast and silent. Above her, she caught only a glimpse of the sun. Feeling a coldness inside, Morwenna shivered. It was a chill she recognized. She had felt it before, but not so strong. It came first when Miss Helga swept up the dust in the palace hallway. It was there again—stronger—when she tried to speak to her mother. It came when the spirits visited her at night. Finally, it came when Swen wanted breakfast and she knew she couldn't wish for that. Now the knowledge that there were only four wishes remaining brought the cold again.

Whenever she came to understand more about

the wishes, that pain increased. It was as if, with the wishes, a shadow, a cold painful shadow, had crept into her heart.

How much—just then—Morwenna wanted the Voice to return and explain to her all she needed to know. It did not. It stayed still. Only to warn her, to guide her, did it speak. Perhaps that's a rule, she thought.

As if to prove the truth of it, the cold and painful shadow grew.

VI

I N the middle of the forest they came upon
an open field. Huts had been built around
the edge where tall trees crowded. Beneath these
trees Morwenna saw a few small fires, some with
cooking pots raised over them. Here and there
old clothing hung to dry.

As she and Swen were led into the center of
the field, people emerged from their huts. Curious, excited, they stared and pointed at Swen
and followed closely behind the swordbearers.
Even if Morwenna or Swen had thought of es-
caping, it would have been impossible. They
were surrounded.

They were led to a hut at the far end of the
field. A man appeared from its doorway. His
cheeks were hollow, his gray hair thin. He leaned

upon a staff. But as he observed Swen, his tired eyes grew bright.

"My name is Gareth," he said at last, speaking solely to Swen. "I am the leader of these people. And you are said to be the Wizard. If you are, and what we've heard suggests it's true, you are very welcome." His voice was full of emotion. "We have waited years for you."

"Years?" said Swen, not sure how to respond.

"Years," Gareth repeated. "Years of great hardship. May I ask you, do you have a name?"

"It's Swen."

"Swen," echoed Gareth, weighing the sense of the word. Then drawing himself up, he said, "Are you the Wizard?"

Swen gave a quick look to Morwenna, then said, "I suppose I am."

"Only suppose?" asked Gareth, taken aback.

Swen shoved his hands into his pockets, flicked his hair from his face. "See," he explained, "I never knew I was. Honest. I mean, it wasn't anything I did. Or planned. Didn't even know about it. It . . . just seemed to happen."

Gareth's puzzlement grew. "But didn't you free yourself from Ruthvin?"

"Yes, sir," said Swen.

"With a wish."

"Nobody more surprised than me."

Gareth, clearly troubled, leaned heavily on his staff and studied Swen for a long time. "Perhaps," he said finally, "we should talk alone."

"If you want," Swen agreed. "But I'd like to have my friend with me." He indicated Morwenna. "Don't do anything without her."

For the first time Gareth considered Morwenna. It was only a momentary look and she saw no real interest in his eyes. "If that's what you want," he said.

"And, sir?" asked Swen.

Gareth turned back.

"We'd like some food. We're really starved."

"First," Gareth said, "we need to talk." He led the way into his hut.

*I*T was dim inside and bare. The old man motioned them to sit on the ground. Then Gareth studied Swen again, as if the boy were a puzzle he had to solve.

"When I was very young—your age perhaps—" he began urgently, "it was my grand-
father who told me that the Wizard has hundreds
of wishes, all he wants, the only ones in the
land. This wizard can do anything with them.
Anything. If nothing hurts him, if he's protected, he can live for countless years. I'm not
the only one who believes these things. Are they
true?"

After a moment Swen said, "I don't know."

"You don't know . . ." repeated Gareth.

Swen looked down as if he had done something wrong.

"Why don't you know?" asked Gareth.

"I told you," Swen replied, "it's all so
new . . ."

"But you do have the wishes?" Gareth said.

"I used them," Swen tried to explain, "a few
times. You said you heard that yourself."

Gareth turned to Morwenna for a moment,
as if to ask whether she'd heard what Swen was
saying. She looked away, not wanting to be
there. It seemed unfair to Swen, to Gareth, to
herself.

Then Gareth spoke again. "Do you hate
Ruthvin as much as we do?" he asked intently,
leaning toward Swen.

"Oh, sure," Swen said, glad to be certain about something. "Doesn't everybody?"

"All of us fled from his crimes," Gareth said. "He's killed those we loved. Family. Friends. He's destroyed our lands, our work. It's he who should be destroyed. And we *have* tried. Tried everything! Once, there was a whole army under my command. Gone. Overwhelmed. Others tried to take back grain he stole, attacking here, there. They were executed." Gareth shook his head. "He's too strong for us. We've had to wait for something—or someone—to make us strong. Now, you've come . . .

"Swen, if you are the Wizard and have the wishes, it's your responsibility to join us. You, as Wizard, are the protector of this land and all its people. Do you understand that? With you among us we cannot fail."

Swen stole a look at Morwenna to gauge her reaction to Gareth's words. When she kept her eyes averted, he returned to staring at the ground.

Gareth reached forward and with the tips of his fingers turned Swen's face up so he could look into the boy's eyes.

"Swen," Gareth said, "I needed to speak with you alone . . . because you seem so unsure.

Don't you see, our struggle against the king has no room for uncertainty. We must act with strength. Are you afraid of being Wizard?"

Swen, after a brief hesitation, nodded yes.

"Because you're so young?" Gareth said, with sympathy.

"No," said Swen. "Not that."

"The power then?"

"Not that either."

"Then what is it?" cried Gareth.

"I tried to tell you," Swen pleaded. "It's all new to me. I'm not sure what to do, not about anything!"

Frustrated, Gareth turned to Morwenna. "He said you were his friend. I must know: is he the Wizard or not?"

Morwenna looked at Swen's open, anxious face. She saw how much he wanted her to agree that he was the Wizard. And there was Gareth, who wanted it just as urgently. But all Morwenna could hear was the Voice calling:

Hide them well. Both you and they.

Before Morwenna could decide how to answer, a woman poked her head through the doorway.

"Gareth," she called, "they've found a beggar wandering in our direction. They're bringing him in now."

Using his staff, Gareth stiffly pulled himself up. "I have to attend to this," he said. "Wait for me here." At the doorway he paused and looked severely at Swen. "You are very young. To raise false expectations is a cruel thing and will not go unpunished. Your youth shall not deter me from my responsibilities."

NERVOUSLY, Swen plucked at his sleeve. "Not much fun is it?" he said. "You'd think people wouldn't fuss so . . . Anyway, I could sure use some food."

Morwenna waited for what he might say or ask next, yearning to find some way to let him know the truth. He must know.

"Look here," he said after a moment. "You want to go home. But he's asking so much, Morwenna. I don't know how I'll be able to do half of what he wants. Or even . . . any. I need your help."

Morwenna saw an opportunity. "Why?" she quickly asked.

"Morwenna, I don't know what to do," he cried. "I'm no good at this." There were tears in his eyes.

"Maybe," suggested Morwenna, "you're not the Wizard."

Swen looked up angrily. "How else did all this happen? Stop making fun of me! You going to help me or not?"

"I'm trying."

"Then do it!"

"Swen," Morwenna began, wanting to scream out the truth. But the moment she spoke, the Voice cried:

Or all shall be lost! All!

"What?" he asked sullenly.

In anguish, Morwenna only shook her head.

"Hey," said Swen. "I'm not asking much. I'm your friend, remember. Least, I used to be."

"You still are."

"Then act like one!" Swen shouted suddenly. In his anger he got up. "I'll get myself some food." He left the hut.

*M*ORWENNA watched Swen from the
doorway. She felt deeply wounded
by what he had said, worse about what she had
not.

Seeking some distraction, she looked across
the field. A crowd had gathered at the far end.
Morwenna stepped out for a better view.

In the midst of the crowd stood the beggar,
a hood partly covering his face. The moment
Morwenna saw him, she sensed he was—or at
least resembled—someone she knew.

Leave! Leave at once!

Morwenna was in no mood to listen to the
Voice. Instead, curious, wanting to get closer
to the newcomer, she slipped among the trees,
then around the edge of the field. Soon she was
close enough to hear Gareth ask the man what
he was doing in the forest.

"The king," was the beggar's reply. "King
Ruthvin. What do you think of him?"

The question made the crowd grow tense.
Gareth stiffened.

"Did I say something wrong?" asked the beggar. His eyes were constantly shifting as if in search of something.

"What made you ask about Ruthvin?" Gareth wanted to know.

"To tell the truth," replied the beggar, "I have been running from the king's soldiers."

"Why?"

"Like you, I'm a thief."

"We're not thieves," Gareth said.

"Forgive me," said the beggar. "I'm only looking for a place to rest. I've been traveling long and hard." Again his eyes searched the field. "It was your people who brought me here. I'd like to stay a while."

"As a thief," returned Gareth, "you're not welcome. As an enemy of the king, our enemy, you are. Stay until you've rested. Then be on your way."

The beggar gave no answer. He merely bowed his acceptance.

Turning, Gareth saw Morwenna. "Where's Swen?" he demanded.

"Looking for food," she said. "He's very hungry."

Irritated, Gareth surveyed the field. The beggar eagerly followed his eyes. Then, remembering himself, Gareth turned back to the man. "As I said, rest. Then go." And he set off to look for Swen.

The crowd drifted away, no longer interested in the stranger. Only Morwenna stayed. She watched the man seek a resting place. The one he found allowed him to look over the entire camp.

He craned his neck. As he did the hood which partially covered his face fell away.

Hurriedly, he drew it back. But his movement wasn't quick enough. Morwenna saw his face for sure: it was King Ruthvin. And she knew why he'd come. He was hunting Swen.

*M*ORWENNA'S first thought was to call out. But in an instant she felt her mind pulled another way, not toward thoughts of saving Swen, but rather toward letting him take care of himself while she ran and hid.

Yet how could she betray her friend? How could she think of leaving without even letting him know or warning Gareth?

Feeling panicky, she searched the field for some sign of Swen. He wasn't anywhere. But she did see Gareth on the far side of the camp. She ran to him.

"Where's Swen?" he demanded as she hurried up. "I can't find him."

"That man," said Morwenna, trying to catch her breath, "that beggar . . . it's the king . . . Ruthvin."

Gareth gasped. "Ruthvin? Here?"

"You must believe me," Morwenna cried. "I see him every day. I know what he looks like. He's after Swen. Look at him yourself." Turning, she pointed to where Ruthvin sat. But he was gone.

"The Wizard!" came a wailing voice. "The Wizard has been killed!" People were running across the field. With Gareth at her side, Morwenna also ran.

Swen lay on the ground before Gareth's hut. His eyes were closed, his face dull white. Blood was spreading on his clothes. Some half-eaten bread lay nearby. He had found some food at last, gone to eat it, and been attacked.

Bending down, Gareth pressed a hand against Swen's heart. "The beggar!" he screamed, springing up, his face twisted in rage. "Catch that beggar. It's the king!"

Some plunged into the woods. Others dashed to their huts for weapons. Most gathered in small, frightened groups. Over and over the words came, "The Wizard is dead."

Morwenna knelt beside Swen's body, searching his face, stroking his limp hand. There wasn't the smallest trace of life. Nothing. She looked to Gareth but saw only horror and shock in his face.

She turned back to Swen, telling herself that his death was her fault, that she should have acted sooner, warned him, made him understand the truth. But Morwenna heard the Voice too, and it was pleading:

Use the wishes well! Waste them not!

She felt as if she were in a vise, and the vise was pressing tighter. Unable to bear it, refusing to listen to the raging Voice, she whispered, "I wish Swen would come back to life."

Not a sound. Not a stirring. But in that silence Morwenna heard an inner silence. There, in that beginning came a single infinitesimal pulse.

In seconds, Swen let out a tiny thread of breath. His fingers fluttered. He opened his eyes. Blinked. Slowly, he sat up.

"Someone," he said to Morwenna, with a shake of his head, "someone tried to kill me." He pushed his hair away from his face. "That's twice, Morwenna."

Morwenna was too overcome, too exhausted to do anything but close her eyes in relief. But she heard a sound behind her, and turned. It was Gareth. He was not paying the slightest attention to Swen. He was staring at her, his look ablaze with understanding. Instantly, Morwenna realized he had heard her wish. He knew the truth.

"And do you know who it was, Gareth?" continued Swen, turning to the old man. "I thought you were supposed to protect me. There I was, finally getting something to eat, when Ruthvin—King Ruthvin—was beside me. Here. Morwenna, didn't I tell you he'd try again? Well, he did. Right by your hut, Gareth."

He stood up and discovered the blood on his clothing. Momentarily puzzled, he put his hand to his chest, then looked at his stained fingers. "You said you wanted to know if I'm the Wizard, Gareth." He held out his hand. "That should prove it. Had to be magic that saved me. I mean, he came right at me with his dagger. Took me completely by surprise. Nothing but magic could have saved me."

Slowly, Gareth shifted his eyes from Morwenna to Swen. He nodded his head. "It's proof enough," he said.

"All right, then," Swen said. "I am the Wizard for sure. And I say we go to the city and take Ruthvin. Give him a little of what he tried to do to me. But, Gareth . . ."

"What is it, Swen?"

"I really need to eat!" With that Swen strode out to the middle of the field. There he was met with cries of astonishment. The people cheered him. They touched his hands. And when he told them he would lead them to the city and help overthrow King Ruthvin, they swept him up and placed him on their shoulders for a grand parade. What did they care that the king had escaped? No matter that Swen was a boy. Full of wishes that worked, he was the Wizard. There was absolutely nothing to fear.

How Swen loved it! He laughed. He cheered them on. "To the city!" he cried. "To the city!" the people shouted back.

Gareth, standing by Morwenna's side, looked on. "They have their wizard," he said to her. "But I have mine."

VII

*F*OR the next twenty-four hours Gareth's
people prepared to leave their field in
the forest. But it was as if they looked forward
to a carnival, not a march against a cruel, enemy king.

Morwenna stayed by the edge of the field and
watched. Gradually, she came to understand
what she had done by saving Swen. Gareth,
she was certain, knew it was she who had the
wishes. Yet Swen believed more than ever that
it was *he*. And more—these people were set to
march to the city because they believed Swen
would make them strong enough to overpower
the king.

How much harm she had done!

But that night, after everything had been made

ready for departure, a great bonfire was lit. Swen was the heart of the party; Morwenna had never seen him so happy, open and free, so sure of himself.

Must she deny him that?

Why were the wishes so hard!

With a start, Morwenna realized that by saving him she had used another wish. Only three were left.

Only three . . .

At once, she felt the cold shadow grow inside. With it came a clutching, sickening pain—the realization that every time she used a wish the shadow would spread, spread until she would be no more. The wishes would be her. She vowed not to use another one. And more. Swen *had* to know the truth.

*A*LL that day Gareth had kept away from her. Now, with the celebration at its height, he came to her side. Leaning on his staff, eyes bright with the reflected light of the fire, he silently watched his people. Morwenna waited, fearful of what he might say.

"Morwenna," he finally began, "it's you who are the Wizard."

The warning Voice spoke too:

Flee! Flee!

"Swen was dead," continued Gareth. "You brought him back to life. It's you who hold the wishes."

Morwenna didn't trust herself to speak.

"It's you we've waited for, Morwenna," said Gareth, speaking softly, but with excitement. "You are the one who can save us from Ruthvin." He smiled. "Is it necessary for me to ask you to do that?"

Morwenna looked at the ground and remained still.

"Did you hear me?" Gareth said softly.

Morwenna nodded.

"Very well, Morwenna. I ask you—urgently —save us."

Morwenna looked up. The way Gareth was gazing at her—as if he were a child and she the adult—made her turn about to see if someone else was standing by her side. No one was.

Hide them well!

"What if it's not possible?" she whispered.

"Not possible . . . ?" said Gareth.

Morwenna shook her head.

"But . . . it must be!" Gareth said, shocked.

"Why?"

"Because you have the power!" he cried. "Morwenna," Gareth went on excitedly, "Swen has told the people he'll lead them to the city and depose Ruthvin. Good. That's exactly what I want. What everyone wants. But . . . if just Swen is there, the king and his troops will destroy us all. Not one of us will survive!"

"Can't you tell them that?" Morwenna said.

"And do *nothing?*" cried Gareth. When Morwenna didn't reply, he turned angrily away and stared at the people celebrating.

"Morwenna . . ." he began, then stopped. Abruptly, he called out. From out of the crowd on the field, seven men ran to his side. Morwenna recognized them as the seven guards, the men who had brought her and Swen to Gareth's camp. Alarmed, she came to her feet.

Quickly, Gareth spoke to the guards, words she couldn't hear. But as soon as he stopped speaking, the seven moved behind her and—at some distance—stood between her and the forest.

Gareth turned to face her again. The softness in his face was gone. "Remember what I told Swen," he said harshly. "It's my duty to protect the Wizard. Very well, let people believe that Swen's the Wizard. What better protection if no one knows who you are.

"Look behind you," he said, and pointed to the guards. "They don't know why, but I've given them strict orders not to let you out of their sight. No, you'll stay with us."

And he left before Morwenna could reply.

⁂ ⁂

⁂

S WEN came next. Red with excitement, glowing with happiness, he threw himself on the ground. "Come on, Morwenna," he said, "you don't have to stay alone."

Morwenna, trying to collect her thoughts, said nothing.

"I know," he said, rolling on his back. "It's hard to believe. But you can't pretend it isn't so. I'm the Wizard."

Still Morwenna said nothing.

"Least you might be happy to see me alive."

"I am happy!" Morwenna cried out, hurt by his words.

"You sure don't act it," said Swen.

"You don't know anything about how I'm acting," said Morwenna, with sudden anger.

Feeling rebuked, Swen was silent a moment. "Anyway," he said after a while, "you've got what you want. We're going back to the city."

"Maybe," she murmured, "I won't go."

Swen sat up. "Short time ago you said you wanted to get back. Now you're saying the opposite. Morwenna, you keep changing! Look here, we started together. Might as well finish that way."

"What is the finish?" she asked sincerely.

"No more riddles!" cried Swen. "I'm done with that. You keep forgetting, I'm the one who saved you when you fell from the cart. I'm the one who got you to the square and freed myself. And these people—I got them to find us. Then I saved myself from Ruthvin again. You know I did. Why do you keep saying I didn't?"

Even as Swen spoke, Morwenna heard the Voice:

Say not who you are or what you have
or all shall be lost, both you and they.

Morwenna swallowed the tears she felt coming. But before she could answer, Swen rose up. "You know what it is?" he said angrily. "You want the wishes for yourself. You're jealous."

"It's not that at all!" cried Morwenna.

"Then what is it?"

The Voice screamed:

Or all shall be lost! All!

Morwenna hung her head.

"Morwenna," said Swen with an edge to his voice she had never heard before, "everybody else believes in me. You're the only one who doesn't. Maybe the inn keeper was right." He started to walk away.

"Swen!" Morwenna cried after him.

He stopped and looked back.

The tears had come. "You are my dearest friend," she said.

After a moment Swen replied, "I don't believe you." Turning on his heel, he rejoined the celebration.

Morwenna felt something sharp and new: bitterness. It made the shadow inside her grow.

She glanced over her shoulder. The seven guards were there, watching. She didn't care. She was determined to escape.

M ORWENNA waited in the hut they'd been given for the night. At last Swen's deep, regular breathing told her that he was asleep. But still she waited, staring into the blackness, trying to find the courage to do what she felt she had to do.

"Swen?" she called softly.

No response.

"Swen . . . ?" she said again.

Certain he was asleep, Morwenna sat up and listened. Other than Swen's breathing there were no sounds. With great care she crawled to the door and pushed away the cloth curtain.

The field, lit by a sliver of moon, appeared empty. She heard crickets, and the stirring of trees in a soft wind. From a distance a night bird called.

Morwenna stood up and breathed deeply. The smell of the rich earth mixed with the sharpness of the evergreens, and the scent of wood flowers filled her, gave her the energy to tell herself she must go. But the dark expanse of sky and forest made her aware of how alone she was.

Once again she struggled to think of some way to tell Swen the truth. How much better if he knew. They could run away together. Now, with everything so changed, she would be happy to stay in the forest. But she was afraid that if she tried to explain they'd only have another argument. She didn't want that again. Ever.

Which way to go? she asked herself. Ruefully, she remembered her joyous thought of a few hours past, the belief that she could go anywhere. The thought wasn't joyous now. Even if there was a right way, she knew she'd never find it in the dark. No, she wanted only to get among the trees. Once there, she would hide. No one would find her.

She tried to judge the shortest distance to the forest, then realized that the hut they had been given was set apart from all the others. Was it a trap?

Quickly, she chose what she thought was the best way and took steps in that direction, only to hear a sound behind her. She turned. Twenty feet away, the form of a man stood up. She whirled about. Another stood, until, in moments, she found herself surrounded by eight men. One of them moved toward her. It was Gareth.

"I am sorry to frighten you," he said softly. "But I gave you fair warning. I will not let you go." He held out his hand.

Morwenna shrank back. "I mustn't stay," she pleaded.

"I am trying to be kind," Gareth said. "If necessary I can be harsh. Please, return to your hut."

By the faint light Morwenna saw his eyes. Hard. Implacable.

Firmly, Gareth turned her around and led her back to the hut. At the doorway he paused. "No one need know but us. All the same, consider yourself my prisoner."

VII

*A*ND where was King Ruthvin?

Certain he had killed Swen—killed the Wizard—he fled into the woods, hardly able to suppress a cry of triumph. By his own hand he had saved his rule.

He made his way through the forest and reached a town, and there demanded respectable clothing, taken the fastest horse and raced to the city and his palace. With unrestrained glee, he informed Sibald of all that had occurred.

Sibald coupled lavish praise for his king with words of caution. "Majesty," he said, "when the Wizard escaped your gallows, the news of what happened and how it happened spread quickly. The whole country believes that the Wizard is among us.

"This news has given rise to a great restlessness. People expect something more to happen. You have destroyed the Wizard, Majesty. But who *saw* you do it? Who will believe their hero is dead?"

"Fools!" cried Ruthvin. "I killed him with my own hands. With this!" He drew out the dagger with which he had struck Swen and pressed the point against Sibald's chest.

"Majesty," stammered Sibald, very frightened and trying to back away, "no matter how much you show that dagger as evidence, people still won't believe you. They *want* to believe in this wizard."

Ruthvin lowered the dagger and became thoughtful for some time. "Then I will do more," he said at last. "I will show them that I had nothing to fear from that boy. Nor do I fear anyone else now. If I need to demonstrate my power again, so be it."

"Majesty?"

"Go out into the countryside . . . take a troop of the best soldiers . . . show yourselves here, there . . . everywhere. At the slightest provocation—no matter how small—react quickly and sternly. Make people understand that I am still the king, that I will sweep aside anyone who so much as appears to stand in my way."

Sibald turned to go.

"Sibald!"

"Majesty?"

"Make sure you *do* find someone who stands in your way. Use him as an example. Do I make myself clear?"

"Yes, Majesty," said Sibald, hurrying out.

Alone, King Ruthvin held the dagger in one hand. Carefully, he placed the weapon in easy reach, beneath the cushions on his throne. "Just in case," he told himself. "Just is case . . ."

*N*EXT morning a royal proclamation was posted by every path and cart track in the country.

<u>THE WIZARD IS DEAD</u>

Be advised! King Ruthvin the Renowned has destroyed the Wizard with his own hand.

To show his might and authority he has sent Sibald, Army Chief, to travel throughout the

land. He shall seek out *anyone* who challenges
the rule of Ruthvin and put him to death. Let
no one stand in his way. Let no one challenge
the King's rule.

LONG LIVE RUTHVIN!

By then Sibald had raced out of the city. With
him went fifty of the king's best soldiers, ready
to strike down anyone who voiced any opposi-
tion.

*F*OR two days Gareth, striding along with
the help of his staff, led his small band
through the forest. Swen walked beside him,
and, a step behind, came Morwenna. On either
side of her, acting unobtrusively so no one would
suspect she was their prisoner, marched the
guards. They spoke to her pleasantly, or to one
another. She hardly talked at all.

Swen was feeling frisky, shying rocks at trees,
laughing, telling jokes, bubbling over with good
humor. He talked about anything that came to
mind. Sometimes it was about his mule—whom

he loved and missed—or his leaky roof at home, which he hated. Sometimes he spoke of adventures he'd had while hauling on the road.

Though Gareth listened patiently, he said little in return. But when, in the midst of his chatter, Swen asked what they would do once they reached the city, Gareth replied, "It depends on how we're met."

"What do you mean?" asked Swen.

"Do you think Ruthvin will just let us march in and take his crown?" Gareth said. "There'll be plenty of soldiers."

"Maybe we don't have to worry, Gareth," Swen suggested. "Maybe when they learn I'm coming, they'll run."

Gareth glanced quickly back at Morwenna. "Perhaps," was his answer.

"And, Gareth," Swen continued, "what happens after we get rid of Ruthvin?"

"That depends on your plans."

"Mine?"

"Do you have any?"

"I'd better find my mule," Swen said. "I keep thinking about all the work I've promised to do. People must be wondering."

Gareth smiled. "Since you're the Wizard,"

he said, speaking so Morwenna could hear, "you can be much more than a mule driver."

"Not me," insisted Swen.

"With your powers, you could become king."

Swen stopped walking. "Is that a joke?" he said.

"Absolutely not."

"King," repeated Swen, astonished.

"The one who has the power has the choice," said Gareth.

For a moment Swen studied Gareth's face to be sure he wasn't being teased. Then he turned to Morwenna. "Did you hear, Morwenna? Me, king!"

*I*T was a day later when the marchers stepped from the protection of the Great Forest. There, at the edge of the trees, they gazed across a flat and barren land which had hardly a bush or hill to break the emptiness.

A road stretched from where they stood to beyond the horizon. The marchers felt dispirited looking at its length. Quickly, Gareth let them know that the road would lead them to villages and towns, eventually to King Ruthvin's city.

"All we have to do," he told them, "is travel across the plain."

"Nothing to worry about," Swen agreed. "If anything happens, we've got my magic."

Someone discovered a copy of the king's proclamation posted to a tree and brought it to Gareth. When he read it out loud, people laughed.

"He thinks I'm dead," said Swen, treating it all as a joke. "Makes me want to get there even more." He hurried to the road eagerly. People hastened after him.

The proclamation had a different effect on Morwenna. To go forward meant she'd be where the greatest danger was. What could happen to her? To the wishes? She feared the answer.

Gareth, watching her, saw her standing motionless. He came to her side.

"What's the matter now?" he demanded.

"I mustn't go on," she told him.

"Morwenna," he began, then stopped and made a sign to the seven guards. They drew closer.

Morwenna stepped back. "What are you doing?"

"Morwenna," snapped Gareth, "you have no choice. Accept that fact."

Morwenna felt an almost irresistible urge to free herself completely by wishing them all away. But no sooner did she have the thought than the cold Voice cried out:

Use them well! Waste them not!

Even the Voice was against her. She felt defenseless.

"Must I force you?" demanded Gareth.

Morwenna tried to hold up her head. "I'll come," she said.

"See that you do," Gareth said. He turned to the guards. "Stay with her," he ordered, then hurried to the front of the marching line.

Morwenna, humiliated by her quick retreat, closed her eyes and took an oath to herself: at the first opportunity—no matter what it cost— she would flee.

*T*HE open road lay beneath a harsh, burning sun. At first the people marched with new energy, but as the sun grew hotter, the air heavier, they began to slow.

Swen and Gareth were kept busy offering words of encouragement, promising the marchers that they would soon be free of the heat, close to the city and certain victory. But as people struggled to keep up, they slipped further and further apart until the line—with many gaps—grew very long.

Morwenna realized what was happening and saw the possibility of escape. Her guards, who where struggling too, grew lax. First one, then the others began to neglect her. Soon she was marching without their company at all. By moving with deliberate slowness, she forced more and more people to pass her by. In time she would be at the end of the line and all alone. Given the right opportunity—with Gareth and Swen so busy with the marchers up ahead—she'd be able to break away. No one would notice.

*I*T was not long before someone at the front of the line saw a cloud of dust in the distance. Gareth brought the marchers to a halt.

Swen thought it was a storm. Gareth was not so certain. For a long while he stood there, watching.

With a frowning glance backward, he took in his bedraggled band. His people—sure Swen would protect them—had left their weapons behind. They were totally unprepared for danger. The only ones who had swords were the seven guards . . . Gareth looked for them, and with a start realized that they were no longer with Morwenna.

"Look!" someone cried. Gareth spun around. It was clear now what was causing the dust: a troop of horsemen was moving in their direction.

A ripple of nervousness passed down the line. Those who had been straggling hurried along, seeking the protection of others. Even the guards, now alert to possible attack, rushed forward, thinking that was where they would be most needed. Morwenna didn't matter now.

As for Morwenna, she was no more certain who was coming than the others. But she saw a chance for escape. She started to move further away from the marchers.

Gareth, caught between apprehension about the oncoming horsemen and concern for her whereabouts, finally noticed Morwenna. She was running away.

"Soldiers!" cried someone.

Once again, Gareth turned to look. The soldiers' helmets and swords were plainly visible.

It was the same cry that made Morwenna stop and look back.

Swen had placed himself firmly in the middle of the road, certain he could block anyone who tried to harm them. "Don't worry," he called out. "Just stay behind me. I'll protect you all."

As Morwenna watched, the frightened marchers crowded into a tight wedge behind him as if he were a shield.

The Voice cried in Morwenna's ears,

Flee! Flee!

Hand to her throat, she forced herself to turn

away from the scene and began to run again.

Gareth saw her. Even as the soldiers drew yet closer, he started to follow.

"Stop, Morwenna!" he cried. "You must stop."

She only ran faster.

Gareth paused, hefted his staff and, using it as a javelin, flung it forward. It flew like an arrow, striking Morwenna on the shoulder. The blow caused her to spin about and fall.

In a moment Gareth reached her and hauled her up by the arms. "Look!" he cried. "Look at what's happening!"

Compelled to watch, Morwenna saw the soldiers press forward at a gallop, their swords raised. She saw, too, that it was Sibald in the lead.

"Surround them!" the army chief cried. And the soldiers spurred their horses on even faster.

Gareth's people tried to flee. There was no place to go. They had gathered together into too small a knot. The king's soldiers, moving to take advantage, surrounded them swiftly. Only Gareth and Morwenna stood outside the ring.

Undaunted, Swen held his ground. "Stop!" he cried. "You mustn't hurt these people!"

The soldiers paid him no attention. Instead, they drove their horses in a smaller and smaller circle so that the people inside it appeared to be bound together.

Swen lifted his hands above his head. "I wish," he shouted, "I wish us all safe!"

Though they heard him, the soldiers didn't so much as pause. "Destroy them!" ordered Sibald. "Every one!"

Crying, "Do something!" Gareth let Morwenna go.

She saw the soldiers with their wild horses and deadly swords threatening the crowd. She saw the people's fear, their desperation.

She opened her mouth, only to feel the press of an invisible hand hard against her lips. With a wrench of her head, she pulled away and called out, "I wish these people saved!"

No sooner did Morwenna speak than from the ground rose a shimmering wall around the marchers.

Sibald's soldiers could not have stopped, even if they'd wanted to. Instead, they hurled themselves and their horses against the wall. With a shattering din their swords splintered, their horses reared. Gareth's people, transfixed, saw that they were safe, and, as far as they knew, it was Swen's wish that had done it.

Outside the wall, the soldiers stared at the stumps of their swords. No one needed to tell them they had been stopped by magic. They had heard Swen's wish. They had seen and felt the wall themselves. As one, they turned and fled down the road toward the city. Sibald was swept along with the rest.

THE wall vanished. All that remained as proof of the marchers' miraculous delivery were bits of swords, torn harnesses, a few battered helmets.

And Swen.

He stood in the midst of the crowd, hands still high over his head, a look of joy on his face. "I did it!" he cried jubilantly. "I wished us safe. We can't be hurt!"

The people laughingly embraced each other.

It was then that Swen saw Morwenna and Gareth standing apart. Wildly excited, he broke from the cheering crowd and ran to them. He swept Morwenna off her feet with a great hug.

"You see!" he shouted. "There's nothing to worry about. I told you I could do it!"

He set Morwenna down and ran back to the others.

"Come on," he called to them. "To the city. To the king!"

Their danger quite forgotten, people began to follow with more confidence than before. Swen was clearly their leader now, and he led them all in a song of victory.

Gareth remained with Morwenna. "You see why you must stay," he said. "Come. You are not badly hurt. I'll tend to your shoulder." Taking her by the arm, he guided her back toward the marchers.

⁂

*T*HE pain of Morwenna's shoulder was nothing compared to the almost unbearable pain within. Utterly exhausted, she felt more a prisoner than ever. And three wishes were gone! With Swen convinced beyond all doubt that he could do whatever *he* wished, she realized that even as she held the wishes, the wishes held her.

*B*Y nightfall they had come through the most barren stretch of their journey and reached a stream. Rain had started; it fell with a constant hiss as they made their camp under the partial protection of a few trees. The fires that people managed to light burned fitfully, the wood spitting and bubbling. Swen, sprawled asleep, lay with his head pillowed in his arms.

Morwenna sat before some weak flames, a blanket stretched overhead, trying to catch a little warmth. Gareth was rubbing liniment into the bruise on her shoulder where his staff had struck her.

"We'll be near villages and towns soon," he said.

Shifting slightly, Morwenna stole a glance behind. The seven guards, though they kept themselves in shadow, were there to see.

"Gareth," she said, "you once told me you knew all about the Wizard. Did you learn how a wizard could give up the wishes?"

"Have all that power and give it up?" he exclaimed with a mocking laugh. "Whatever wizards are, they shouldn't be fools." He patted her shoulder. "By morning the redness will be gone." He took a place by the fire and held out his hands to warm them. His eyes became sad.

"Morwenna," he said suddenly, "I don't understand you. What I do know is that with one wish you could set yourself—and all of us—free. And yet you resist. Why? If you wanted, you could take care of . . . everything. Instantly. You must have reason for not doing it.

"One wish . . ." he said to himself, looking steadily into the fire. Abruptly, he turned to her. "How many do you have?" he asked, his voice hard. "Five hundred? A thousand? That's what I was told. Morwenna, get rid of Ruthvin and you're free to go. You know perfectly well what he's done, how many he's killed, made to suffer. What more does he have to do before you use your power? Don't you see how selfish it is for you not to use at least one of your wishes? One, Morwenna, one out of so many!"

Even as Morwenna felt tempted by what Gareth was offering, she began to hear the Voice:

Hide yourself and the wishes well,
for when they are gone, so shall you be.

Morwenna stopped listening to Gareth's words. The Voice's words echoed in her mind:

When they are gone, so shall you be.

For the first time she fully grasped the meaning of the words: that when the wishes were gone, she would die.

"If I had what you have," continued Gareth, unaware of her thoughts, "I wouldn't be so cruel. Look at you," he said accusingly. "How old are you? A child. Who gave a child the right to choose? Who are you to be so above the rest of us? Above me? It would have been much better for me to be the Wizard. I know what's important. Why should you have the power when I'm the one who's struggled for so many years. Morwenna," he cried out to her. *"Listen* to me!"

"Do you like riddles!" asked Morwenna.

"Riddles?" he said, exasperated. "What has that got to do with anything I said?"

"I have a riddle for you, " she continued. "Try and guess. When dark, it's bright, when brightest, it's gone. When gone for good, so will I be. — What am I?"

Gareth studied the fire, as if the answer were there. He looked up at her and smiled knowingly. "A shadow?" he said.

"No," Morwenna replied. "A wish."

"That makes no sense to me," said Gareth.

124

"What if there aren't a hundred wishes?" Morwenna suddenly said, unable to keep inside the turmoil she was feeling. "What if there are only a few?"

Instantly, the Voice began to shriek into her ear:

Hide them well! Hide them!

"Morwenna," said Gareth, "if there were only one wish, *one*, and I had it, I'd know how to use it. Get rid of Ruthvin. Why don't you?"

With his hard eyes on Morwenna, Gareth sat there, waiting, demanding an answer.

All Morwenna heard was the Voice:

Or all shall be lost. All!

When she didn't give Gareth an answer, couldn't give him one, he got up and moved away.

❋
❋

*F*EELING more alone than ever, Morwenna listened to the rain and watched the smoldering fire. Deep within she felt the fountain of fear that was her pain. She recalled how at first she had believed she could do anything with the wishes, that everything was in her reach. Now she saw that it was as if a wall of impossible choices had been built around her. How bright the promise of the wishes! How dark the reality! How much she wanted to tell someone what had happened, what she had become. But there was no one to tell except the Voice.

"I don't want the wishes," she whispered to the dark. "Take them back. Find someone better than me to have them. Someone older. Wiser. Stronger. Someone who wants them. Take them back and let me be what I was. Or is *this* my time? And is my time my end? Please, I beg you. I must know!"

She waited for an answer.

Rain fell. The fire burned down. Swen continued to sleep. The Voice stayed absolutely still.

IX

WHEN they fled, the king's soldiers would go nowhere but back to the city. Sibald, who was greatly frightened himself, was happy to agree. It was urgent that he speak to King Ruthvin.

The boy who had routed them had acted like a wizard, had even made a wish. If he was the Wizard, the same one pronounced dead by the king, people would believe the boy invincible. Surely there would be an uprising. Moreover, the road this boy and his band were traveling led directly to the city. Might they be coming to *attack* the king?

With all this in mind, Sibald ordered his solders—on pain of death—to tell no one what had happened. As an extra precaution, he waited until late night before allowing them to enter the city gates. Even then he had the horses hooves wrapped in burlap so they would not be heard on the old stone streets.

Once in the barrack, he again threatened his men about keeping their silence. Then he hurried to the king.

THE weary soldiers pulled off their boots and armor and cast their broken swords away. No one spoke. No one offered to play cards or share a drink. Instead, they slipped out of the barrack one by one, until a single soldier remained.

He had been with the king when Swen was first arrested. He had held Swen's arms, and was one of the men who led the boy away. It was he who, while standing on the gallows, read the document proclaiming that Swen held traitorous magic. He had seen the bird free Swen. And finally, he had ridden with Sibald and crashed into that extraordinary wall. The man was shaken to his soul.

"Is mine a special guilt?" the soldier asked himself. Would the young Wizard—so powerful, so indestructible—seek him out to punish him in particular? "And how long," the soldier asked himself, "will the king last?" Was there anything he himself, a simple soldier, could do to gain forgiveness?

Dressing quickly, he crept into the dim city streets, anxious to reach the safety of his own room. It was already past midnight and the way was dark and empty. The only sound was his steps. Or was it? He stopped, listening to some vague stirrings. Was he being followed? No, it was only a cold wind gliding through the city. Even so, he realized he was trembling with fear. And again he asked what he could do to rid himself of his sins against the Wizard? He remembered Sibald's warnings, not to tell anyone what had happened.

He had to do something.

Looking about and seeing no one, he picked up a white rock from the street and went to the nearest wall. There he began to scratch a *T* on the stone. No sooner did he start than he felt a tug on his hand, some force trying to keep him from writing. More determined than ever—

using two hands to grip the rock—he wrote:

THE WIZARD IS COMING!

When the soldier finished, exhausted, the tugging ceased. Only a moaning, weeping wind remained. It brought a new chill to the man's heart. He began to run and didn't stop running until he was safely in his room, the door bolted shut.

❋
❋

Sibald had gone directly to the king and told him everything that had happened.

"But I killed the Wizard!" Ruthvin insisted. "Killed him with my own hands!"

Sibald described Swen.

"It is him," the king was forced to admit. "Something has brought him back to life. He was dead when I left him."

"Majesty," Sibald said, afraid to speak his own thoughts, "what will happen if people know he's alive and coming in this direction?"

King Ruthvin, shaken, retreated to his throne,

trying to think. The Wizard was far, far more powerful than he had ever imagined. The wishes did seem to make him invincible.

Bitterly, the king reflected again that those wishes had been offered to him. Now it would take all his cunning to keep his throne. "I should have taken those wishes," he lamented, "those five . . . wishes."

Suddenly, an idea began to form. "Sibald," he said softly.

"Majesty?"

"When I first met the Wizard he offered to give me . . . five . . . wishes. Only . . . five. He said that they . . . were all the wishes left. All . . ." he mused. "*All!*" He sat up straighter as his excitement grew. "Sibald," he cried, "the Wizard made a wish to save himself from the gallows. No! He used two wishes."

"I don't understand," Sibald said.

"First, he wished that someone would come to see him. I don't know who. No doubt that person appeared. Then, it was the *second* wish that brought that bird. And surely," the king said, more and more pleased with himself, "he must have used a wish to save himself when I stabbed him."

Ruthvin reached down behind the cushions of his throne and touched the dagger, as though to reassure himself.

"That's *three* wishes! Now, you tell me he saved his army with yet another wish."

"I heard him make one," said Sibald.

"Therefore," cried the king in triumph, "he has used *four* wishes. He has *one* wish left, only one. What we must do, Sibald, is make him use that last wish."

Sibald, impressed with the king's reasoning, made a deep bow.

Ruthvin felt bold and sure of himself once more. "Sibald, drive from the palace anyone you suspect is not loyal to me."

"It will be done, Majesty."

"Let the Wizard have the city," said the king. "I shall stay here. As long as I hold this fortress, I will hold the crown. Bring me every soldier you can trust."

"Yes, Majesty."

"Close the gates, Sibald. Lock them tight. No one is to enter or leave. *No one!*"

"Done, Majesty."

"Post sentries at every high point. If there is the slightest suspicion that the Wizard is coming, send for me instantly. What I shall do,

Sibald, is force him to use his last wish. Once he is powerless, then I am safe. Now, go . . . No, wait! One final thing. Do all this as secretly as you can and without explanation. The longer the people in the city know nothing of what we protect ourselves against, the less they hear about the Wizard, the better for us."

Sibald went to do as he was told.

*T was a beggar prowling the streets in search of food the next morning who first noticed what the soldier had written on the wall. Deciphering the words, the man felt a sudden stirring of hope.

THE WIZARD IS COMING!

Rummaging in a pocket, he pulled out a bit of chalk. And he repeated the words on yet another wall around the corner.

THE WIZARD IS COMING!

The beggar went on, writing the same message over and over. Within a few hours, the entire city knew.

THE WIZARD IS COMING!

✳
✳

E VEN beyond, in the countryside, people knew. The closer Swen and the marchers came, the faster the news spread. More and more people joined them. First one or two came along. Then they came in groups. Soon they came in throngs.

Swen welcomed each and every one, promising two things: that they would overthrow the king, and that he would protect them all.

Soon the marchers were no longer Gareth's little hungry band. They had become an army, Swen's army.

✳
✳

U RGED on by her guards, Morwenna moved forward as if in a daze. The words, *two wishes left*, came like drum beats in her head. She kept thinking of Gareth's suggestion, too, that one wish would resolve everything. But how was she to know what was truly worth a wish? The fewer wishes she had, the more important the remaining ones became.

She, with so little knowledge, experience or understanding, what did she know of what was best to do? As bad as Ruthvin was, mightn't there be something worse the very next day?

She, who had so far used the wishes to save life, did she have the power to *take* it? Was that, too, to be her right, her choice? The idea that it was seemed unthinkable, terrifying.

She, who was not allowed to talk to anyone about the wishes or what she was, or what she felt, how was she to do it all alone?

Two wishes left.

And every time she made a wish—a wish that at the moment seemed right to make—her predicament grew worse. The fewer wishes there were, the closer she came to the end of her own life.

Two wishes left.

Nor could she choose whether to go to the city or to run away. Gareth had made sure of that. Clearly, he meant that she should use her wishes as he saw fit, for the freedom of the country.

But what about me? Morwenna felt like crying out. *What about me?*

✤
✤

*B*Y early evening, the army reached the crest of a hill and saw the city. The marchers stood and stared. "So many houses!" cried one of them. "So many people!" said another.

"And," added Gareth, "so many soldiers."

"Don't worry," Swen assured him. "I'll take care of them with my magic."

Morwenna saw the city, too. But her sense of danger had become so constant, her pain so much a part of her being, that she saw much more. For even as she saw the lights of the city, she saw where the light ended, where the dark engulfed the light.

✤
✤

*T*HE marchers camped by the side of the hill. Later that evening, when Gareth, Swen and Morwenna had finished their meal, a man approached. He bowed and bobbed his respect, then began a little speech. "Honored sirs," he said, "A delegation has come from the city."

"From the king?" asked Gareth, quickly rising to his feet and smoothing down his hair.

The messenger shook his head. "The king is locked up in his palace. These people want to speak to the Wizard."

For a brief moment Gareth's and Morwenna's eyes met, then Gareth stepped aside and pointed to Swen. "He's the one you want."

Swen stood up.

There were four people in the delegation. They had tried to be festive and had pinned a few ribbons to their clothing.

"Are you our wizard?" one of the people asked Swen—an old and toothless man.

Swen said he was.

With much whispering and pushing, a woman from the group was made to come forward. She began with a bow. "Sir," she said, "we've been sent by the city people. We're here to welcome you." She bowed a second time. "We've waited a long time for you, sir. Can't begin to tell you how glad we are that you've come at last and we're going to be done with Ruthvin.

"All you have to do," she went on, "is get rid

of him for good. That should be easy enough for you. And then, it's you who can have the crown. You can be our king. We'll put our trust in you."

Behind her, her companions burst into applause.

Swen stood his place. To Morwenna he looked no different than he had ever looked, tall, boyish, but now so very proud of himself. With a twist of his head, he flicked the hair out of his eyes. "Tell them," he said, "that when I get rid of Ruthvin, I'll accept the crown."

*I*N the middle of the night, Morwenna stole away from the encampment. Everyone appeared to be asleep, but she was sure that Gareth and the guards would be awake. All the same, she picked her way between the quiet figures around her, and started up the hill. She didn't go far before Gareth showed himself.

"I need a moment alone," Morwenna said wearily, before he could speak. "I'm not running away."

"Do I have your promise?" Gareth said.

"Yes."

"I will be watching," he warned her.

Morwenna made her way to the top of the hill.

On one side of her lay the hundreds, the thousands now, who had joined the army. In the other direction lay the city and the king. Above, was the great web of stars. Around her, the Voice throbbed:

Two wishes left! Two alone!
Hide them well! Hide them well!

Tomorrow, Morwenna knew, it might all come to an end.

"I tried to do what was best," she said to the air. "I tried to learn. I didn't have much time and I wasn't given many wishes. If I must have them, if they must be mine, if at the end of the wishes I am to die, then please, I beg you, give me more of them!" And then she said, "I wish for five more wishes!" But the Voice said only:

Two wishes left. Two alone.

Morwenna understood: she could wish nothing for herself.

And tomorrow they would march into the city.

X

*T*HAT morning Miss Helga woke up a very cross woman. Morwenna had not appeared in many days. The chamber maid was willing to accept one day's absence—even two might be excused. If Morwenna was ill, her friend, Swen, could have brought a message from her mother. As it was, her bed at the far side of the room remained untouched. Miss Helga might have rented it to someone else. Without so much as one word for so many days, she felt her anger was justified. Her patience was at an end. Morwenna had taken advantage of her fondness.

As she ate her breakfast, Miss Helga tried to think of other things. There was much to choose from. The city was tense, full of rumor. She had heard reckless whispers about a great wizard who was coming to depose Ruthvin. Then came word that this wizard had been killed by the king himself. After that there were excited rumors that the Wizard, far from being dead, was leading a mighty army to oust the king.

Some said King Ruthvin had fled. Others claimed he was hidden in the palace. Wasn't the palace locked up tight? If only someone had asked her, she could have told them the truth. Miss Helga, who had her own way to get in and out, had seen the king in the palace only the day before. He was more pensive than usual perhaps, but he was there nonetheless.

Miss Helga, with her practical mind, considered it all of little matter. Kings might come and go. Dust remained. What mattered was that Morwenna had left her with too much work to do alone.

*P*ASSING through the city streets that morning, Miss Helga felt the tension in the air. Crowds of agitated people milled about, whispering. On the walls, here, there, everywhere, rough letters proclaimed:

THE WIZARD IS COMING!

And when she reached the palace she found—as had been the case for a number of days—the gates locked tight. It was all a bother. As if such things could keep her from losing her pay! Not Miss Helga. She made her way to the old, forgotten porter's entrance and let herself inside without anyone noticing.

As she bustled through the palace, she saw great numbers of soldiers, all fully armed. And all were tracking mud everywhere.

And there were sentries, too, perched at every high point, staring out over the city. Other soldiers paced battlements bristling with bows and arrows. Let them pace! She didn't have to clean there.

Miss Helga set about her chores. She knew they would take her from the palace basement right to the king's own throne.

How she wished Morwenna would come! In her head Miss Helga rehearsed her scolding speeches.

*B*y the time Swen's army reached the city gates it numbered many thousands. Theirs had ceased being a march. Now it was a parade. While most walked, others ran. Children darted in and out. Old people made their way with confidence. Some marchers were on crutches.

Swen, in the lead, was like a child with too many toys. He wanted to gather in everyone he saw, welcome them, make sure they were all his friends. Shaking hands, kissing babies thrust at him—he touched them all. And constantly, people cried out with joy, "The Wizard! The Wizard has come at last!"

A step behind Swen came Gareth, keeping a tight hold on Morwenna's hand. Behind her were the ever-present guards. Morwenna, pulled along, felt as if she were in a dream, numb with dread at what would happen.

*T*HEY moved through the city gates into the city proper. Swen's smile grew ever more radiant. He looked exactly as people wanted him to look. Never mind that he was fourteen years of age! He was the one who would set them free. His eyes sparkled with laughter. His blond hair, his tall bearing—everyone noticed it, approved of it, felt blessed by it. Oh, wonderful wizard to have come to them at last!

If before he had been pressed by admirers, now he was besieged. On the walls crowded hundreds, thousands. They shouted. They cheered. They hung from windows. They stood on roofs. They clung to every sign and post. Waving, shouting, cheering. Horns blew. Drums banged. Whistles shrieked. How wildly happy everybody was. Not a window, not a doorway, was unfilled. And, no sooner did Swen pass by than those who had been watching, joined in. This army, rolling forward, grew in size and might as every moment passed. The city, beneath its steady tramp, shook with excitement.

Oh, Swen, Swen the Wizard!

*F*OR Morwenna, every face was a plea, every cheer a cry, every reaching hand a fist upon her heart. Shouldn't she wish the outcome? Shouldn't she give the people what they so dearly wanted? Didn't they have the right to it? But even while the great crowd roared its hopes, Morwenna heard the Voice:

> *Two wishes only! The only ones left.*
> *Waste them not. When they are gone,*
> *so too shall you be.*

Show me some way to live! Morwenna cried inwardly to the Voice. Give me some way!

But no answer came.

Instead, the number of people expecting—demanding—victory grew. And Morwenna was swept along.

*O*N the walls of the palace, the waiting soldiers were at first surprised, then astonished at the number of people who began to crowd toward them through the city streets. And shortly they saw that at the head of the vast army was Swen. They sent for the king.

One look was enough. "That's him," the king snapped at Sibald.

Instantly, he ordered the warning alarm rung. As it tolled, he and Sibald climbed the highest tower, from which they could see the palace battlements, the courtyard, the gates.

Sibald, too frightened to say a word, simply stared down at the swelling mass of people outside the walls.

"Once we have made him use that last wish," said the king with assurance, "we shall be safe. Absolutely safe."

SWEN led his people as far as they could go, close to the palace walls. There he stopped. Every eye was on the fortress now, tall, dark, built of heavy stone. On all its battlements armed soldiers waited.

Swen looked back to where Morwenna and Gareth were standing.

"Think it's time?" he shouted over the din.

Gareth gave Morwenna's shoulder a squeeze as if to pass the question on to her. When she said nothing, he nodded yes to Swen.

For a brief moment she saw Swen hesitate. His old self. A spark of hope gave her energy. "Swen!" she cried.

Their eyes met.

"Don't do it!" she pleaded.

Swen's eyes hardened. As he turned away, Morwenna's heart sank. She began to tremble.

Facing the fortress, Swen took a step forward and lifted up his hands. The great crowd hushed itself. Above, the soldiers strained to look and listen. The entire world seemed to be holding its breath.

"*R*UTHVIN!" cried Swen, his voice echoing over the thousands of upturned faces. "Ruthvin!" he cried once more. "My name is Swen . . . and I . . . I . . . I am the Wizard!"

A cheer rose up, booming like a gigantic beast.

"Ruthvin," Swen cried again, made bolder

by the great voice at his back, "you are not wanted in this land. Everybody wants you to open up the palace gates. And I agree. Let us— let me—inside. Can you hear me, Ruthvin? Open up the gates!"

Once more the crowd let out a roar. The air shook with it. "Swen!" the people began to chant. "Swen is king. Death to Ruthvin. The Wizard is king!"

❀
❀

*K*ING Ruthvin, looking down, heard the cries of the people roll up again and again. And he gave the command for his soldiers to draw their bows.

Five thousand soldiers plucked arrows from their quivers, lifted their bows, notched arrows to strings.

"Ready!" cried Ruthvin, looking down again at countless upturned faces.

The soldiers drew back their bowstrings.

The great crowd below, seeing what was about to happen, shouted out their angry defiance.

"Shoot!" cried Ruthvin.

Five thousand arrows, each one tipped with sharp, blackened steel, each one a slender slash against the sky, flashed into the air.

The people, alarmed, began to push back, trying to escape the rain of arrows. It was impossible. There were far too many of them crowded together. They were trapped.

❈

*M*ORWENNA was afraid to look. Afraid not to. She knew the bloody result if she didn't act. But there was the Voice, too, wailing:

Waste them not! Waste them not!

Her hands pressed to her ears, Morwenna cried out, "I wish the arrows would turn to dust."

The terrified people gazed spellbound as the arrows turned in the air, twisted, became a mist and disappeared. From the great crowd a voice rang out. "Magic!" came the cry.

As one, the people took up the word. "Magic!"

they shouted in unison. "Magic! Magic! Magic!"

The soldiers watched in awe from the battlements. But Ruthvin, above them on his tower, turned to Sibald with satisfaction. "We are saved," he said. "There are no more wishes left."

*I*N the midst of the roaring crowd, Morwenna saw nothing but darkness, heard nothing but the Voice, soft and weeping:

Keep it safe, both you and it. Keep it safe, that one last wish. When it is gone, so too shall you be.

She opened her eyes. Gareth was looking at her with relief, nodding his heartfelt satisfaction. At that moment, Morwenna hated him as she had never hated before.

*T*HE crowd had been happy, festive. But the ugly violence of Ruthvin's arrows changed that. It made them realize that the king would use all his power against them. The Wizard—with his magic—was their sole protection.

Now grave and watchful, the people waited to see what would happen next. Every eye—save Gareth's—was on Swen.

Swen himself stood perplexed, unsure what had happened or why. Since it was something magical he believed he had done it. How else could it have occurred? He had no other explanation, so he shrugged aside his puzzlement and again lifted his arms.

"That was just a warning, Ruthvin," he shouted. "Open the gates. If you don't, I'll make another wish!"

The word *wish* was instantly caught up. A hissing chant began. "Wish it! Wish it! Wish it!" Every word seemed a blow against Morwenna, a demand for her life. And it only grew louder.

*H*IGH on his tower, King Ruthvin was certain he was safe. "Shoot again!" he commanded.

But that time, when the soldiers reached into their quivers, instead of arrows they found dust. In all the city, not one arrow remained.

THE panic began with a soldier who stood inside the fortress, guarding the gates. He knew what had happened. Like others he had heard Swen's threat to use more magic and had reached for his arrows as Ruthvin commanded—only to find them dust. Unable to control his fear, the soldier threw down his bow and his sword, and began to run.

By ones, by twos, by hundreds, the soldiers fled the fortress, unable to move away fast enough from the Wizard and his wishes. The king's army, in a stampede to save itself, evaporated within moments.

Those who remained tried to gain favor by opening up the palace gates. At the sight, the crowd beyond the wall let out a triumphant roar of victory.

Swen turned to his people. "The palace is ours!" he shouted. "Find Ruthvin!"

The return cry was instantaneous. "The Wizard is king. Swen is king!"

*M*ORWENNA tried with all her strength to stand against the press of the crowd. It was too powerful. Within seconds she was shoved aside. But the force of that shove caused Gareth to lose his grip. Morwenna pulled away.

"Swen!" Gareth shouted. "Morwenna needs you!"

Swen heard Gareth's call. He spun about and saw Morwenna push into the crowd. Thinking she was in danger, he reached out and grabbed her hand. "Hold on!" he cried. "I'll protect you!"

Desperately, Morwenna tried to free herself. "Let me go!" she screamed. "I'll die! I'll die!"

"Don't worry," Swen shouted over the roar of the crowd. "We're winning!"

"You don't understand!" she screamed back. "You're not the Wizard. You're not!"

"Trust me, Morwenna, trust me!"

The people had reached a state of near wildness. They exploded forward toward the palace gates, overwhelming everything that stood in their way. The terrified soldiers scattered, ripping off their armor, crying for mercy.

Swen, pushed as much as he led, dragged Morwenna along. "We've almost won, Morwenna. We've almost won!"

XI

*K*ING Ruthvin and Sibald saw the soldiers melt away, saw the gates flung
open, saw that there was no stopping the people. Sibald was too frightened to move. But
Ruthvin grabbed hold of him. "Nothing to worry
about, Sibald. There are no wishes left. Follow
me."

They dashed down the stairs and into the
throne room—where they discovered Miss
Helga. She was on her hands and knees, scrub-
bing the floor.

King Ruthvin rushed past her without a word
and hurriedly settled on his throne. He ordered
Sibald to stay close. "Do whatever I tell you to
do," he whispered. "I'll show these people there
are no more wishes."

Miss Helga, realizing that something unusual was happening, struggled to her feet. Mumbling a quick apology, she turned to leave. The great doors broke open before her.

※

*P*EOPLE poured into the throne room. Swen, still holding Morwenna, came first. Behind them the rest pressed forward, eager to see the confrontation between Ruthvin and the Wizard. In their midst was Gareth.

Ruthvin wrapped his royal robes around himself and sat tall upon the throne. Sibald, nervous and scared, hovered close by.

Swen had never been in the throne room before. He gazed about, fascinated by the wealth and splendor of it.

As for Morwenna—she could think only that she had returned to the place where it had all begun, and where it would most likely end. Within her, the incessant Voice demanded, ordered, pleaded, begged that she act, do something to free herself.

Miss Helga stood amazed. Seeing Swen in front of the crowd was astonishing enough. But seeing Morwenna—she was dumbfounded. Nonetheless, all the anger she had been feeling jumped out.

"Where have you been!" she cried to Morwenna. "Why haven't you sent word? Swen," she scolded, "you might have had the good sense to keep me informed. What is this all about?"

King Ruthvin, who had been staring hard at Swen, turned to Miss Helga. "Do you know these people?" he demanded.

"Yes, Your Majesty," the chamber maid answered. "That's Swen. He's a mule cart driver. And that's my helper, Morwenna. She works in the palace, too. At least," she said with a flash of anger, "she did work in the palace for me. I'm not sure I want her anymore. She's not very reliable."

But having blurted her angry words, Miss Helga became embarrassed, realizing how foolish she must appear, talking about such things in such a situation.

"Forgive me, Your Majesty," she said hurriedly. "I don't know what this is all about. I should be going." And she made a move toward the door.

"Stay where you are!" cried the king. "I decide whether anyone goes or not!" He turned to Swen. "You there," he said, "you claim you're the Wizard. She says you're a mule driver."

Swen, whose confidence was somewhat shaken by the king's show of authority, tried in spite of that to stand proudly. "I am the Wizard," he answered. "Ask anyone."

"What makes you think so?" pressed the king, seeing a way to provoke him. "I choose to believe her."

"But I have the wishes," said Swen.

King Ruthvin smiled, sure he was making progress. "Do you?" he said. "How many do you have?"

"Many," replied Swen. "As many as I need."

"When I met you," said the king, "right outside these doors, you said you had only five wishes. The last five."

Swen gave a vigorous shake of his head. "I never told you anything of the kind. And I've got all the wishes I need. Don't I?" he suddenly asked Morwenna. "Tell him!"

"What's that girl to him?" King Ruthvin quickly demanded of Miss Helga. "Why did he ask her that? What does she know about it? Why is he holding her?"

"They're friends," returned the chamber maid, with an apologetic glance at Morwenna.

Suddenly the king knew the way to provoke Swen. "Sibald," he called. "Seize that girl."

Alarmed, Morwenna tried to break away from Swen, who, distracted by the king's questions, had let his grip slacken. She pulled free, only to run into the crowd pressing from behind in hope of seeing what would happen next.

Sibald took a step toward her.

"Go on!" urged Ruthvin.

Swen now moved forward. "Keep away from her," he warned Sibald.

"Do as I tell you!" raged the king, delighted that Swen was reacting. "Arrest her instantly."

As frightened of Swen as Sibald was, he was just as afraid of Ruthvin. He took another step.

"Do as I command!" cried the king.

"I can't" cried Sibald, unable now to make himself move.

"Then I'll get her myself!" screamed the king. Ripping his dagger from its hiding place among the cushions, he jumped down from the throne and moved toward Morwenna.

"Don't you!" warned Swen. "I'll use my magic!"

Ruthvin taunted, "Use it, if you have any!" And he lunged forward. Even as he did, Swen flung himself in the king's way. He took the blade in his heart and fell to the floor.

Morwenna cried out.

Ruthvin gazed coldly at the boy sprawled before him. "There's your wizard," he said.

With a scream of outrage, the crowd leaped forward, knocking down both Ruthvin and Sibald. Within moments, both of them were dragged from the throne room, prisoners of the people.

*A*s far as the crowd was concerned, the great struggle was over. King Ruthvin was toppled. The Wizard had sacrificed his life to bring them their freedom. They rushed from the throne room to spread the news. Even Miss Helga, mumbling words of apology, hurried away.

All that remained were Morwenna, who knelt beside Swen's almost lifeless body, and Gareth, who looked on.

S WEN'S eyes were cloudy and beginning to close. "Did they . . . take . . . the king?" he asked with effort.

"Yes," Morwenna whispered.

"Is it done . . . then?" he said.

Again Morwenna whispered, "Yes." She cradled Swen's head in her lap.

"Don't worry," Swen managed. "I'll wish . . . myself better. I will . . . Everything will be . . . fine. We'll be friends . . . again. The way . . . it used to be. You can tell riddles . . . and I'll never guess . . . the answers. Right now . . . I'm wishing myself better . . . I . . . am."

Morwenna looked up at Gareth.

"Morwenna," he said. "Wish him alive."

Swen smiled. "You've got it wrong . . . Gareth . . . It's not her . . . it's me . . . I . . . have . . . the . . . wishes. I'm . . . the Wizard."

"Save him, Morwenna," cried Gareth. "As you did before."

"I'm trying . . ." whispered Swen, his voice fading. "I . . . am . . . try . . ."

What Morwenna wanted more than anything was to use the wish to give Swen back his life. But the Voice said:

You are the wish, Morwenna. The wish is you.

For the first time Morwenna recognized the Voice. It was her own. And hadn't it always been? For she was the Wizard. To use the last wish to save Swen meant her death and the death of wishes, too.

"Morwenna," urged Gareth, "wish Swen back to life. Hurry."

The room was very still. Morwenna was crying. She shook her head. "No," she said. "I must . . . I want . . . to live."

And even as she held him, Swen died.

XII

❦

*F*ROM all over the country, people traveled toward the city, hurrying to celebrate the end of Ruthvin's reign. And they came, too, to pay their last respects to the great Wizard, Swen, the boy who had given his life for them.

Against this tide of people a young woman made her way, moving gracefully but with steady steps. She walked neither as fast as she could, nor as slowly as her companion would have liked. For with her was an older man who moved with difficulty, a staff in his hands, trying to keep up.

"You're going in the wrong direction!" people kept shouting to them as they passed.

But Morwenna and Gareth continued on,

journeying for three days and nights until they came to a river. It was there, at dusk, on the third day, that Gareth announced, "I can go no more."

ROM the waters a sweet cool mist rose, seeming to melt the languid, liquid branches of the willow trees.

Morwenna and Gareth looked at one another.

"Then it's time to say goodbye," she said. "You should go back. You could become king, Gareth. You'd do it well."

Wearily, Gareth shook his head. "Let those who know less, do more," he said. "That is usually the way. But," he asked anxiously, "where will you go?"

Morwenna smiled at his concern. "I'll follow this river, I suppose." She could not see where it came from or where it led.

"And then?"

"I don't know."

"Must you? Is that what wizards must do?"

Knowing she could not answer that question, Morwenna kept still.

Then Gareth gathered his courage and said what he had meant to tell her ever since they'd slipped unnoticed from the palace. "Morwenna," he said, "I now understand what Ruthvin meant at the end. You must have been given only five wishes. The *last* five. Believe me, I didn't know. And you've used four, I think. That leaves only one. Am I right?"

Morwenna said nothing.

"Forgive me" whispered Gareth. "I thought I was doing what was right."

Morwenna stayed still.

"People will learn the truth, Morwenna," Gareth said. "They'll find you, force you to use it just as I made you use the others. Then it will be gone. Let me come with you," he said timidly. "I can help protect you. I'll tell no one. I'll make no demands."

"Is it me or the wish you are worried about?" Morwenna asked gently.

Under her level gaze Gareth hung his head. "The wish," he said. Then he looked up. "It's the *last* wish, Morwenna. The only one in the land!"

For just a moment Morwenna thought of her home, of her mother. She thought of Miss Helga. She thought, too, of Swen. "It's safer if I'm alone," she said.

"What if people need the wish?" Gareth pleaded.

Morwenna looked at him and smiled. "If wishes can be found, people will look." Then she turned and started off. "Goodbye," she called.

"Morwenna!" cried Gareth. "Will you let people find you?"

Momentarily, Morwenna paused. But when she realized she didn't have an answer to Gareth's question, she continued on her way.

THERE, THAT IS THE STORY.
So many, many years ago. But I am still
Morwenna. And I am still the Wizard.
That last wish remains in me.

Now my time has come. Must the wish
die with me? Or will you keep it longer?
You know the rules. Oh, they are
very hard. Not just for you. For everyone.
Now, decide . . .
Do you want the wish?